EPIPHANY

BOOKS BY NICKOLAE GERSTNER

DARK VEIL
LONGBOURN

BOOKS CO-AUTHORED BY BARBARA PRONIN
AND NICKOLAE GERSTNER
WRITING AS
BARBARA NICKOLAE

FINDERS KEEPERS

TIES THAT BIND

Reviews

Dark Veil
"Dark Veil takes exciting twists and will keep readers guessing until the last page. A great read.

Catherine Nelson, Rave Review

No Bed In Deseret
"A good read that's also unconventional and moving."

West Coast Review of Books

Ties That Bind
"Readers who dive into this lively story may not want to surface until the end."

Publisher's Weekly

Longbourn
Lively characters, a convincing plot, and humor that would set Jane Austen laughing."

Madeline Baker
New York Times Best-selling author

Finder's Keepers,
(Reader's Digest condensed book selection, translated into 14 languages.)

"It's my kind of book…a neat, suspenseful plot about the kind of people you worry about, written with skill."

Tony Hillerman

"Emotionally gripping. I loved it from the first page."

Mary Higgins Clark

"Nickolae's first novel displays ingenuity and daring.

Publisher's Weekly

"An unusually expert and clever work…plotting is ingenious, eminently readable and suspenseful."

Charles Champlin, Los Angeles Times

"Well drawn and believable. A splendid read."

Baltimore Sun

ISBN: 1516839358

ISBN 13: 9781516839353

Library of Congress Control Number: 2015913035

Createspace Independent Publishing Platform

North Charleston, South Carolina

ACKNOWLEDGEMENTS

Ruth Gerstner for editorial
assistance
and to the Reverend T.P. for valuable advice
and input

Cover illustration by

Michael Wheary
Calypso Concepts

TO JOHN WITH LOVE

EPIPHANY

BY
NICKOLAE GERSTNER

CHAPTER 1

Philip Rockcastle recognized the anxious voice and knew what to expect.

"I've done wicked things, terrible things, but it's not my fault. Ricky is after me all the time. Other people chase me, too. They hide in my bedroom."

Sounding like a quote from an erotic novel, Leonard Wilson continued. "I am forced to disrobe. They gently caress my body. Passion consumes me."

His voice pitched higher. It was time to rein him in. Philip rarely called a penitent by name. In this case, it was appropriate. "Leonard, I've told you that indulging in sexual daydreams can be a sin, but more important--"

"Father, believe me," Leonard blurted. "Everything I'm telling you is true."

"Did you make an appointment at the family services clinic I told you about?"

"I was afraid, and Ricky didn't want me to."

Philip often saw Leonard wandering alone through the neighborhood and suspected he was the young man's only lifeline to reality. He felt a commitment and couldn't cut him off.

"Leonard, I'll make the appointment for you. Counseling can help you understand that these experiences only happen in your imagination."

"Father, you're wrong! They really happen."

"Listen to me. You imagine these things. They're fantasies, daydreams."

"No! They are real! Why won't you believe me? I need someone to believe me. No one listens. No one pays attention to me."

Leonard's voice quivered. He was on the edge of tears. Philip realized he had pushed too hard. He was a priest, not a psychiatrist. He backed off, quickly giving Leonard a penance and blessing.

Leonard was always the last penitent on Saturday evening, obviously waiting so he could delve into fantasy for as long as possible. Philip had just played into his game by reacting. He resolved not to let it happen again.

Leaving the confessional, Philip paused at the altar. He had been called to the priesthood not once but twice. The first time he had been very young, solemn in his determination to spend his life serving God, and certain nothing would ever deter him. He had been wrong. Another life had loomed, unexpected and irresistible, but that life vanished in a cloudburst. Afterward, angry and confused, he had drifted for several years until a renewed desire to be a priest guided him back to where he belonged.

Leaving the church, he paused to put several misplaced hymnals back in their rack. God's house had to be kept tidy, but at home Philip had a talent for clutter. The cleaning woman managed to keep the rest of the rectory neat, but his desk was usually covered with an assortment of mail, bills, and an occasional slip of paper where he'd jotted a name or phone number and couldn't remember why.

Philip pulled the heavy church door closed behind him and turned the iron key in the lock. His LeBaron was parked in the back lot at a sign that read *Pastor Philip Rockcastle*.

At forty-two, he was young to be a pastor and was aware his more staid parishioners might wonder at their priest driving a red convertible. The car had come his way when his brother decided it was time for a newer model, and Philip enjoyed driving it.

After retracting the top, he drove a short distance to a sprawling park. He had a rare few hours to himself and took a leisurely drive down a tree-lined road, enjoying the balmy aftermath of an unseasonably hot September day. A tangy wind blew in his face as he drove around the large lagoon. It was just dark enough for the moon to cast a glowing sphere on the water.

Lights blazed from the windows of the recreation center. Like the rest of Humboldt Park, the center was the scene of many activities, wholesome and otherwise. The sight of police cars was not too surprising.

An officer standing in the road signaled to him, and Philip pulled over. "Father Rockcastle." Making the name a greeting, the officer approached the car. "We have the road blocked up ahead. You have to turn around."

"Tom, what's the problem?" Philip asked. They had played on the same softball team at a parish picnic and enjoyed a beer afterward but, despite Tom's smile of recognition, their camaraderie was stilted. He was always Father and regretted that he would never be called Philip, let alone a casual Phil.

"A body was found in the center." Tom said. The sight of the clerical collar made people willing to give up secrets and, leaning into the car, he confided, "Looks like a homicide."

"A homicide," Philip repeated, shaking his head. Although always ready to serve the needs of his parish, he didn't have to worry about a murder. He could never be involved.

Circling his way out of the park, he decided it was still early enough to pay Tara DeVeccio a quick visit. She was raising two young boys in a difficult situation. He was concerned and checked on her occasionally. It was not unusual. He was concerned about many of his parishioners.

She lived on the upper floor of a two-story cottage, typical of many neighborhoods on Chicago's northside. Parking was always tight, and Philip was pleased to find a convenient spot. He backed in and, waiting for the top to rise, touched the little silver cross hanging on a chain around the rearview mirror. The moment of prayer was comforting, but he locked the car. God could not be made responsible for sporty cars left unlocked in a big city.

Feeling no need to advertise his presence, he kept his head down and followed a gravel path into the backyard. He climbed the stairs quietly, not wanting to arouse the first floor occupant. She was Tara's former mother-in-law and blamed Tara for her son's abandoning his family for carefree comforts with another woman.

When Tara opened her door, he started to apologize for not calling first. She interrupted. "Father, you know you're always welcome. This is a nice surprise."

"It's no surprise, Father. Mom said we would probably see you tonight. That's why we have cannoli." The back door opened into the kitchen, and the boy pointed at a domed cake plate on the Formica table.

"Derek, that is not true!" Tara said, blushing. "I hadn't made them for a long time, that's all."

Had he mentioned to her that he might have free time on Saturday? Perhaps he had. He couldn't remember, and he reminded himself that he had gone to the park first.

"I bet it's a year since I had cannoli," he said. "I hope my name is on one."

"Absolutely," Tara said. "The one on top has Father Rockcastle written on it." They both laughed. It was silly, but to Philip it was the most refreshing moment of the day.

She poured coffee. Derek got milk out of an old refrigerator, and Tara put cannoli on three small plates, first putting a small paper doily with lace edges on Philip's plate.

"Only three?" Philip asked. "Where's David?"

A frown swept Tara's face. Their eyes locked, and he knew. Her younger son was downstairs with his grandmother.

"She insisted on it," Tara said, her voice a half-whisper. "She fills his head with all kinds of nonsense about why his father..." Pausing, she glanced at Derek. "It's bad for them, but if I'd refused to let David go down, she would have had a screaming fit."

With Derek at the table, they couldn't talk freely, not that it mattered. Philip was familiar with the situation. Tara was a nurse and trying to get enough money together to move. Meantime, she had to put up with the senior Mrs. DeVeccio's verbal abuse and interference with the boys. Derek was eight and David six, impressionable ages, and he knew Tara worried about her for-mer mother-in-law's influence.

She was seated across from him. Leaning back, she closed her eyes--warm brown eyes. Philip had accidentally noticed the color. She seemed tall even to his six feet but once, standing side by side, he had realized she barely reached his shoulder. Her walk and car-riage added the illusion of several inches. She kept her hair long. It was very dark, almost as dark as his. It fell into soft waves around a face he thought many men would consider pretty.

Derek was munching the last bite of his cannoli and reaching for another.

"Derek, be polite. Wait until Father has another one."

Derek waited, his hand poised over the cake plate. "Come on, Father. Take yours."

"Yes, Sir," Philip said in mock deference as he served himself. "Tara, they're delicious. I would say they were better than my mother made, but she never made them."

"If your mom never made them,' Derek said, talking and chewing, "my mom's have to be better."

Derek was never without a response, a bit of a rascal, but Philip thought he was an exceptional boy.

The kitchen was old-fashioned, like something out of a 1960s TV show. Tara had added colorful touches including a clock that whistled a bird tune on the hour. It was a relaxing place, and they always had an easy time talking. Religion was never a topic. In one of their early conversations, she told him she was not a devoted Catholic. "I like the church, and I take my boys," she had said, "but I'm open to other ideas." He had let it go at that.

As soon as Derek finished eating, he jumped up, headed toward the television, then spun around to give a belated, "Excuse me."

"Tara, you need to move," Philip said when they were alone. "This is not a good place for you."

"I know, Father, but every time I think I'm going to have enough money, something comes up and wipes me out. I told you my transmission is acting up again."

Cheap rent with former in-laws had a financial benefit, but Philip doubted it was worth the strain. "If things here get too bad, you have to let me know. We'll manage something."

For a moment, they were silent, then she said, "David will be disappointed he missed you. Can I tell him when you'll come again?"

Before Philip could answer, she continued. "I'm not working Thursday. I'll have time to do up a big lasagna. Maybe, I can tell David you're going to help us eat it."

Philip thought a moment. "I didn't bring the boys the DVDs I have for them. I might be able to bring them on Thursday."

When he left, Tara called after him. "Thursday, Father. Don't forget."

The combination of God and the lock had protected his car. The door wasn't jimmied, and the hubcaps were where they belonged. He got in but didn't drive away. Sitting quietly, he looked back at the house. A light came on upstairs, in the front where a bedroom had to be. A shadow passed by the window. It was too tall for either of the boys. He continued watching, waiting for the shadow to pass by again.

His muscles tightened. He jabbed the key into the ignition. Leonard Wilson was lying to himself. So was he.

CHAPTER 2

At Mass the next morning, Philip made the usual announcements and added that the first of an annual series of religion
classes would be held Wednesday evening. The classes were also
mentioned in the weekly bulletin and on the sign in front of the
church. Beyond that, Philip never advertised. He had faith that
the people who should hear, would hear.

He liked to start the series in September, the month when
most people remember returning to school. Only about three or
four people showed up when he first started the classes, but they
had grown each year. Lately, close to a dozen people usually
attended. He held the class in the rectory. With his desk wedged
diagonally between two walls, he had room in his office for as
many fold-up chairs as needed. The arrangement could be a little

close at times, but Philip felt it created a more relaxed atmosphere than meeting in the church.

Philip was glad that for the next two days he had a fuller than usual schedule. Not until he was setting up chairs for the Wednesday class did he allow Tara DeVeccio into his thoughts. He had known a momentary confusion, but was not in love with her. He was certain he wasn't, and he would never go through that door. She was alone and needed his advice and encouragement. It would be wrong to end their friendship, but he would be careful to make their relationship more formal, perhaps by encouraging her to attend the classes. It would reinforce that he was a priest; this was his life. He didn't love her. She must never love him.

Nick Crane was the first person to show up for the new class. Philip was not glad to see him. With a wave in lieu of a greeting, Nick strode into the office, took the chair farthest from the desk and leaned back, letting his chair bump the wall. His deep, blue eyes had a fierce intensity and, although probably in his forties, he still had thick, white blond hair. His appearance said laborer, but Philip knew he had a sharp, agile mind that delighted in the devious.

Nick's wife was a devout Catholic who worried that her non-Catholic husband might not make it into heaven, depriving her of his company for all eternity. In less Christian moments, Philip wondered why the thought distressed her. The man's hobby was being confrontational, and he excelled at it. Although his attending religion class occasionally might be intended to appease his wife's doubts about his post mortem adventures, it was more likely, he came because he enjoyed the intellectual challenge of stumping Philip with difficult questions.

A young couple arrived. Had they been twins, they would have appeared conjoined, but they did manage to ease away from each other enough to take touching chairs, Philip recognized the man as a regular at Mass and was confident the pair had the sacrament of matrimony in mind.

Several more people arrived--a few newcomers and an older woman who had attended previous classes. Mrs. Novak always sat with her hands folded in her lap, looking enraptured at every word Philip said. He had been gratified until he realized she was almost totally deaf.

It was not going to be a large class. He had begun explaining the routine when there was another knock. Going to the door, he found a girl, maybe eighteen or nineteen, standing rigid on the threshold. For a moment, he was sure he knew her. Taking a second look, he realized he was mistaken and asked if she had come for the class."

"I saw a notice."

He beckoned her inside, but she didn't move. "It's safe," he said, smiling. "We don't lock you in."

She stared at him, a strange look on her face. "Who are you?" she asked,

She sounded anxious, and he gave her what he hoped was a reassuring smile. "I'm Father Rockcastle. If you want to attend the class, it's this way."

She hesitated, then followed him to the office. Edging passed the lovers, she took a seat, partially blocking Nick Crane from view. That was all right. Nick's sardonic little grin could get annoying.

Philip held up a sheet of paper. "It helps if I know your names, so sign this if you want to." He did not demand names, aware that some people feared if they identified themselves, their names might be put on a nonperishable list of prospects to be virtuously hounded.

Philip continued talking while the paper was handed around. When it was returned to him, he read the names aloud. In scrawling letters, the girl had written *Jane Doe*.

When Philip said her name, Nick piped up with, "Miss Doe, you're too pretty to belong on a slab."

The girl seemed very tense. Nick's comment wasn't going to help her, but unwelcome comments were Nick's specialty. Philip had once considered asking him not to return and had planned to couch it tactfully:

Nick, you are too advanced for this class. Instead of returning, let me get you some reading material that I think you'll find informative.

Philip had banished the thought. Nick would not have been fooled and would have gone away victorious. Philip was not ready to be vanquished and comforted himself with the hope that Nick might be more interested in the church than he let himself realize.

Instead of sitting behind his desk, Philip leaned against the front, his arms crossed, his long legs stretched in front of him. Conducting the class was one of his favorite activities, and he wanted a friendly, casual atmosphere. Every session either brought a few people into the church or helped someone return after a hiatus.

"Any questions before we begin?" he asked.

Jane Doe raised her hand. "How old are you?"

He smiled. "Old enough to vote," he said, handing out booklets that introduced the catechism.

Not bothering to raise her hand again, Jane Doe asked, "How long have you been a priest?"

He didn't like personal questions. They hardly contributed to the subject matter, but he answered: "For eleven years. It used to be that after only eleven years, a priest would rarely be a pastor, but there were more priests then."

Nick called out, "Fewer men are becoming priests because of all the scandals."

Ignoring him, Philip flipped open one of the booklets, and read several paragraphs. He did not take his public speaking skills for granted either here or in the pulpit. This evening, his efforts seemed to be working. He had everyone's attention, except for the lovebirds. They seemed fixated on her left hand. Either it was sprouting extra fingers or was newly adorned with a ring.

Philip couldn't let it go unnoticed. "Are congratulations in order?" he asked.

They nodded. Even their blushes seemed synchronized.

Watching young lovers stirred a memory. For a brief moment, Philip allowed himself to remember. "We all congratulate you," he said catching himself, "and wish you God's blessings."

Except for an irreverent comment or two that Philip refused to notice, Nick kept quiet for the rest of the class. Philip checked the time. It had been almost an hour. He rarely let a class go longer. "Until next week then," he said. "I hope you all return."

Jane Doe stood up when the others did but didn't move toward the door. She was obviously troubled, and her signing with an almost certain alias was suspicious. Again, he had a vague, gnawing feeling that she was familiar.

"Would you like to talk to me? Maybe there is something I can do for--"

Before he could finish, she gave her head a violent shake and dashed out.

He started to go after her, but stopped. If he seemed too aggressive, it might keep her from coming back. She had struck a strange chord with him, something deep and personal. Several times, he had caught himself staring at her. She was thin — probably too thin — -and her hair was pulled back tight, adding to a tense expression. She hadn't asked any more questions, but had twisted in her seat and chewed at her nails. Watching her leave, he hoped he would see her again.

Nick Crane lingered. Philip was prepared for a new skirmish but not for what was coming. "Did you hear about the murdered guy they found in the park a few days ago? I heard on the local news that the cops are bragging they solved the case quick. Hell, they didn't solve it. The guy showed up at the station and confessed."

"Is that so?" Philip said vaguely, continuing to arrange his notes in a folder. His desk might lean toward chaos, but he his class materials had to be kept in order.

"He's that odd-ball kid who roams the neighborhood. They said he fingered his accomplice."

Philip looked up, suddenly uneasy. "What kid? Who do you mean?"

Nick shrugged. "His name is Lenny. Leonard something."

Leonard something. Leonard Wilson. Leonard Wilson had confessed to a murder.

Leonard Wilson liked to confess.

CHAPTER 3

Nick relished his role as a trouble maker but didn't Come across as either stupid or a liar. It had to be true. According to a television report, Leonard Wilson had confessed to the Humboldt Park homicide.

Incredulous, Philip prodded Nick for more information, but Nick shrugged. "That was about it, except they're still trying to ID the dead guy."

The moment Nick was out the door, Philip hurried to his computer for a quick, on-line search: *Humboldt Park homicide; unidentified body.*

Unidentified body yielded entries, some with pictures of the deceased, but nothing recent was linked to Humboldt Park.

Leonard was his parishioner. More than that, he had tried to counsel him. Philip felt a connection, a responsibility, and was too impatient to wait for news. Dodging traffic, he ran mid-block across North Avenue to a convenience store. Snatching a copy of the *Sun-Times off the rack*, he didn't wait to get it home. Spreading it on the counter, he scanned pages until he found the single column article:

Body Found in Humboldt Park

Police announced that the unidentified man found dead in the recreation center, was a murder victim.

Two boys, ages 11 and 12, reported finding the body in a storeroom not open to the public when they trespassed to look for a basketball.

One of the boys told a reporter he initially thought the body was a dummy. He said, "It was kind of sitting against the wall, with his head bent over his knees. He had on a big hat, and there was something red, like maybe a scarf, around his neck. A basketball was right by him. One of his hands was on it. When I saw the hand, I knew it was a real dead person, and we ran."

The article continued with a request for anyone who might help identify the victim to contact the police. The paper was an early edition, no mention of Leonard.

Philip had never inquired if Joe, the grim man standing arms-crossed behind the counter, was the owner of an employee. He worked late hours, and many nights Philip had bought cigarettes from him just before he pulled the heavy iron gate across the front of the store.

Accepting payment for the paper, Joe tapped the door of the cigarette case, his hand seeming deliberately to line with the Marlboros.

Marlboros, that had been Philip's brand, and his gaze stopped momentarily on the red packs. He had been a smoker much of his adult life, usually lighting up almost a pack a day, except for the forty days of Lent when he swore off cigarettes as his self-imposed penance. He had felt bound by the commitment, but the agony of withdrawal was so severe that during Lent last year he had decided to give up cigarettes permanently. One major wench was better than enduring it fresh every spring.

His last pack of cigarettes was still in the refrigerator. When the cleaning woman had asked if she should throw away those old cigarettes, he told her he was saving them. Keeping cigarettes handy, yet not smoking, convinced him he had defeated nicotine.

Returning home, he walked a block to the corner, crossed with the light, and dropped the newspaper into a recycle bin. The summer temperatures that had lingered deep into September were making a quick retreat, the city's notorious abrupt change of weather. The chilly wind felt refreshing, and he lingered outside before unlocking the front door.

The phone was ringing.

"Father, it happened."

"Mike?"

"Yeah, it happened an hour ago." He was having a hard time getting the words out, but Philip understood. Mike's father, an old man comatose for days, had finally released his scant hold on life. In his hospital visits, Philip had comforted the family in their agonizing wait. Sincere words had come easily then; they came easily now. It was different for the death of a person in the fullness of life. There were times when words did not exist. Philip knew that, in grief, faces could approach and moving lips could make sounds as meaningless as the rustle of dead leaves.

Now words were useful. Philip stayed on the phone until Mike sounded comforted. "I'll get with your family tomorrow to schedule the funeral," he said, ending the call.

It was almost time for the ten o'clock news. Although anxious to hear the details of Leonard's confession, Philip knew the young man could not be guilty. The body had been discovered before Leonard left the church, and he had not entered the confessional with murder on his conscience: *Forgive me, Father, for the sins I may have forgotten--like killing a man.*

Certainly, it was possible for penitents to omit sins deliberately, but that could not be the situation here. Leonard's mind lingered in a shadow world. He confessed to make the shadows real. If Leonard now claimed a murder, it was another delusion, hopefully one that would get him needed psychiatric treatment.

Psychiatry was not Philip's domain. It was not his job to analyze penitents who came asking for God's forgiveness, but he had tried to lead Leonard into the real world. He worried that Leonard had sought validation elsewhere because his priest would not believe his fantasies. Sexual exploits would not interest the police, but a murder had been handy.

Philip switched on the local news in time to hear two long commercials, then an on-site report of a serious traffic accident. There was an ongoing investigation into a police shooting. The teacher's union said a strike was imminent, and the Senate had approved the appointment of a Chicago judge to the Supreme Court. Philip was getting impatient when he finally heard a brief mention of the Humboldt Park murder.

The reporter was standing on California Avenue the east border of the park. "The victim is still unidentified," she said, "but Leonard Wilson, a twenty-five year old man who resides in the area, has confessed to his involvement. He named Fedrico Haldero as his accomplice. Wilson is known to have worked in a concession in the park and would have been familiar with the recreation center where the body was found."

Leonard's confession was bogus, but Philip understood that the police had to take it seriously until they checked the facts. As for Fedrico Haldero, Philip had never heard of him--or had he?

He always put everything he heard in confessions out of mind. Now, he struggled to remember. Leonard had mentioned someone who hid in his bedroom. Philip thought the person was a myth, part of Leonard's sick thinking, but what had Leonard called him? Closing his eyes, he ran through the alphabet. *R* seemed significant. He repeated it several times. It came to him: Ricky, a possible nickname for Fedrico.

Perhaps, Leonard had heard rumors on the street tying Haldero to the murder and put himself into the action. It was possible, but the longer Philip thought about it, the less plausible it seemed. Fedrico Haldero was more likely someone who had wandered into Leonard's delusions than a killer.

The phone rang. It was Don Cianca, a former seminarian who had come within a year of ordination before he left to marry. He then sired children who filled a font pew at Mass every week. When they lifted their bowed heads, they could see their father appeasing his unmet goal of becoming a priest by serving as a deacon. Although appreciating Don's help and devotion to the church, Philip did not need his constant reports about every scrap of parish news. This time, Don's news earned his attention.

"You know Leonard Wilson, don't you, Father? He's a tall, overweight blond kid, in his twenties and--"

Philip interrupted. "Don, I know Leonard. I know he's in police custody."

"Right. He and Fedrico Haldero killed a man and--"

"Hold on!" Philip snapped. "Leonard claims to have killed a man. Let's wait until the police had a chance to investigate before reaching conclusions."

"Well, Father, I've heard that the Wilson kid liked to follow Haldero around, kind of hang out with him. People think the murder was probably Haldero's idea, and he got Wilson to help him."

"You're saying they were actually friends--there was a connection between them?" The snap in Philip's voice was gone.

"That's what they're saying. Leonard belongs to our parish, so I thought you should know."

Philip had Leonard pegged as a loner. His dramatic sexual encounters with Ricky were fantasy, but if Leonard and Haldero were known to hang out together, it might give Leonard's confession credibility, at least to the police.

Philip did his best thinking when walking, and he paced from the living room to the kitchen and back again. Instead of clearing his mind, it made him feel like a hamster on a wheel. Pausing, he looked out the window but couldn't focus. He had been confident law enforcement would evaluate Leonard as a mental case, not a criminal. After listening to Don, he wasn't so sure.

Again, the thought gnawed that his efforts to help had backfired and sent Leonard to a place where his confession might be believed. The more Philip considered it, the more troubled he became. It had been more dangerous than ridiculous for him to try to give psychological advice to anyone as disturbed as Leonard. God knows what could happen now.

Pacing didn't help. Looking out the window didn't help. He needed to pray for guidance for himself and the police, but not yet.

The cigarettes he took out of the old pack were brittle from age. Flakes of tobacco fell as he turned on a burner, leaned over the gas range, and lit up.

CHAPTER 4

Attendance at Mass was small the next morning, typical for a weekday. Most of the faces were familiar. When the Mass concluded, Philip went to the door and greeted people as they left. A visibly distraught woman hung back, waiting to be last. When he extended his hand, she grasped it tight in both of hers.

"Father, please, I talk to you."

She was too distressed for a conversation on the steps of the church. "Go to the rectory," he said, pointing. "The cleaning woman is there now and will let you in. Tell her I said you can wait in my office."

Twenty minutes later, his vestments removed and wearing a pullover sweater, he entered his office carrying a mug of coffee. The woman sat on the edge of a chair, clutching a large, multi-colored handbag. She appeared to be in her forties. Her Hispanic face would have been handsome without the worried expression.

Philip held up the mug, by way of an offer.

She shook her head.

Sitting down behind his desk and setting the mug aside, Philip asked her name.

"I am Lydia Garcia. Father, I don't come to the church so often. But my son, he needs help. I have no money, no place to go, nobody to care."

"How can I help him?"

"The police took him to jail. They say he did a murder."

Philip was routinely consulted about myriad problems. Marriages and funerals were his calling. Domestic disputes and even violence came his way for help, as did unemployment and financial despair. This situation was new. Never before had he been asked to assist an accused murderer. "What is your son's name?" he asked.

"Fedrico Haldero."

Even though their last names were different, Philip should have been prepared. He wasn't. It took a moment, then he said, "He has a nickname." It was more statement than question.

"We call him Rico, but his friends—everyone—calls him Ricky. This loco fella tells the police Rico made him help kill a man."

Don's phone call might have raised doubts, but Philip still suspected that her son's guilt existed only in Leonard's fantasy.

Much as he wanted to comfort her, he couldn't explain that. His suspicions hinged on what he knew from hearing Leonard's confession. He could never tell what he had heard or, in this case, hadn't heard. All he could do was encourage her. "Senora, I'm sure if your son is innocent--"

She interrupted with a sharp, "My Rico is innocent!" Gesturing with both hands, she leaned forward and her handbag slipped to the floor. "Rico is a good son. He is a good big brother to his sisters."

Abruptly, she sagged back in her chair. "He had trouble with the police one time. He didn't do so good in school, but now he signed up--he is supposed to start on Monday."

"Start what?"

"A class for drawing. He loves to draw and he draws good. Everybody says it." Unexpected pride edged her voice.

"I will pray for you and your son and ask God to--"

"Pray for him!" she blurted. "That's okay, but do something. You are a man of God. You can find somehow to help Rico."

Philip shook his head. "There's nothing I can do."

"Go to the jail and talk to him," she said, leaning toward him. "When he tells you he is no killer, believe him and tell the police. Make them believe it."

"Senora, I'm sure the police will do a thorough investigation. When they find out Rico is innocent, they will let him go," he said, trying to sound positive.

"They will find out and let him go," she repeated. "Father, *will* they find out? Will they let my Rico come home?"

He couldn't answer. He expected the police to discover Leonard Wilson's confession was just a new adventure in a sick mind, but he couldn't blandly promise her everything would come clean in the wash. His effort to sound upbeat faded. "Senora, there is nothing I can do personally. Have faith. God will protect your son."

She leaned down to pick up her handbag and was slow to sit up again. When she raised her head, her expression had changed. She had looked tense, now her face sagged and she looked defeated. Her lips twitched, seeming not so much like silent prayer as talking to herself in private worry.

She had come to him for help. Even if time would correct the mistake that put her son behind bars, he wanted to do something for her now. "Do you know the police station where they took Rico?"

Blinking, she seemed to refocus. "Two big cops just come banging in and took him when he was eating. I don't know where they went."

"I'll phone the local station. If he is still there, I'll try to see him."

Walking her to the door, Philip said, "Trust God, and everything will turn out all right." Except for a nagging uneasiness, he believed it.

The rest of the day's calendar was full--first a hospital visit, then meeting with Mike's family to schedule his father's funeral. It was late afternoon before he had a chance to drive to the police station on William Avenue. Humboldt Park was probably in that station's jurisdiction. If Haldero had yet to be transferred to county jail, it was where he would most likely be. Philip didn't phone first. An in-person request and a collar were more likely than a call to get him a meeting.

Two officers, a man and a much younger woman, were at the reception counter. When the woman looked at Philip, her aggressive expression didn't soften. Prisoner or priest, it made no difference. Her expression said she could be hostile with anyone.

The male officer's name badge read Sergeant McAdams. Philip tried for a more encouraging reaction from him. "Well, hello there, Mac," he said, opening his eyes wide in surprised recognition.

"Father! Good to see you," the sergeant said, apparently equally skilled at faking it.

After a friendly round of how-have-you-beens, the sergeant asked, "What brings you down here?"

"A parishioner asked me for help. Her son is in trouble, and I promised to visit him."

"She thought he was here in the lock-up?"

"She doesn't know. His name is Fedrico Haldero."

"Whoa! I'll say he's in trouble. We thought we'd have a better shot at a confession if we interrogated him here, but he goes to county in the morning. My guess is he's on hold for a murder conviction."

"May I see him?"

McAdams looked doubtful, and Philip didn't wait for a refusal. "Mac, I promised his mother. I hate to break a promise."

Five minutes later, he was in an oppressive room with a single window too high to see out of and too dusty to permit much suggestion of light. Fedrico Haldero sat across from him at a partitioned table. He was good-looking, almost classic featured. His dark, wavy hair was uncombed but trimmed. A male officer was inches away, leaning against the wall, relaxed, but attentive.

"Rico, your mother asked me to come and see you," Philip began. "She thinks I may be able to help you."

"Help?" Rico said, his tone sneering. "What can you do for me?"

"Maybe nothing, but your mother thought if you told me--"

"No way! She never sent a priest to get me to confess to something I didn't do."

"I'm not here to get you to confess. I'm here to help you if I can. If not, at least I can tell your mother I saw you."

"Yeah? So what's my mother's name?"

"She told me it was Lydia Garcia." Picking up on the reason for the question, Philip said, "She has a big handbag with lots of bright colors, doesn't she? The colors are why I noticed it."

Rico's expression changed. He still looked wary, but the hostility was gone. "Hey, Father, I thought those guys sent you. They were at me for hours, wanting me to admit I killed someone. They kept waving Wilson's confession at me and — "

Philip seized on it. "They showed you his confession? Did you get a chance to read it?"

"I tried not to look at it. Every time I saw my name I got fucking mad." Stopping, he gave Philip an uneasy look.

Philip waved it off. A little street language was not an issue.

"Tell me about Leonard's confession. Did you read all of it?"

"Yeah, and one big ass of a cop kept reading it to me, like maybe if I heard it enough, I'd remember."

Philip said, "Rico, I want you to think very hard. Tell me what the confession said as exactly as you can."

"Hell no! I didn't do it! I don't want to be telling what Leonard said and make it like I can remember. That little shithead followed me around. I felt kinda sorry for him. Then he said stuff like he thought we were some kind of weirdo fags."

Rico winced in disgust. "I threatened him good and told him I'd kick him inside out if he didn't stay away from me."

Philip considered asking for privacy that, in deference to his priesthood, would probably be arranged, but then thought of something handier. He started coughing. The coughing became a gagging fit. "Water," he said in a hoarse whisper. "Please, I need water."

"Sure, Father," the guard said, heading for the door. "I'll get some from the cooler."

"Quick, Rico. Tell me everything you remember from Leonard's confession."

"It just said, well--that we killed this guy."

"We don't have much time. Tell me the rest of it."

Suddenly, Rico sat upright, obviously understanding Philip's need for water. "He said we shot him in the storeroom of the rec center where people aren't supposed to go."

"Did he say how the body was left?"

"Yeah. He said after we shot him, the guy was kind of sitting against the wall with his head bent over on his knees. A basketball was right by him, and his hand was on it."

"More," Philip demanded. "I have to hear the rest of it."

Closing his eyes, Rico looked pensive. Philip also tried to remember. "Rico, did Leonard's confession say anything about what the man was wearing?"

Rico opened his eyes. "He had on a big hat, and there was a red scarf or something around his neck. They told me they knew I took the guy's wallet. The shithead didn't know what I did with it and — "

"Here's your water, Father."

Philip nodded thanks and took a quick gulp. "Rico, when I talk to your mother, was there anything else?"

"Nothing else," Rico said, locking eyes with Philip.

Philip nodded. Of course, nothing else. Rico had read Leonard's confession and so had he. He had no more doubts. Rico was innocent. Standing up, he held out his hand. "I'll let your mother know I saw you."

Despite handcuffs, Rico grabbed his hand in both of his, just as his mother had. "Father, I believe you. You'll help me." Suddenly, he looked younger, a frightened boy, and he was right.

Philip would help him. He had a personal responsibility and had to help him.

Passing the desk, Philip gave the sergeant a farewell wave.

McAdams called to him. "His partner came clean, but this guy is holding back." The sergeant's pink cheeks puffed in a smile. "Did tell him confession is good for the soul?"

CHAPTER 5

Philip didn't need to write down Rico's description of the murder scene. It had already been written. He had read it and had to read it again. At home, he looked for the newspaper, then remembered he had tossed it in the recycle bin. No point trying to retrieve it. The bin would either have been emptied or, more likely, stuffed with more garbage than recyclables.

Without taking time to play the messages on the answering machine, he headed back to the liquor store. "Last Wednesday's paper — -is there a chance you still have a copy?"

Joe eyed Philip from beneath drooping lids. "Padre, the vendor takes old newspapers when he leaves new ones. Wednesday's papers are out of here unless you're after the crossword puzzle." A smirk played his mouth. "They might keep your mind off cigarettes,"

"No crossword puzzles, Philip said, too preoccupied to mind Joe's smirk. "I'm after something that was in the news."

He still had time to get to the library before it closed. If he didn't find the newspaper there, he would try phoning the newspaper office.

Leaving the store, he heard Joe call. "Not very likely, but..." He beckoned Philip inside. "The gal who helps out afternoons likes to do the crossword. She leaves the paper a mess, but she does a good job cleaning the coffee pot."

Amused at the juxtaposition, Philip followed Joe to a back room where boxes of merchandise crowded most of the floor space. An unadorned bulb hung above a wooden table next to a three-legged stool. Joe pointed to the jumble of papers on the table. "Take a look if you want."

Philip rifled through the papers, checking date lines and captions. A bank robber had been caught--a grandmother with no priors. A date had been set for swearing in the new Supreme Court justice. The mayor had called for an investigation of police misconduct. Philip wasn't sure he was checking the right edition until he read, *Body Found in Humboldt Park.*

"It was kind of sitting against the wall, with his head bent over on his knees. He had on a big hat, and there was something red, like maybe a scarf, around his neck. A basketball was right by him. One of his hands was on it."

Philip hooked his foot around a leg of the stool and dragged it toward him. Half-sitting, half-standing, he leaned his weight on the table and studied the article, acknowledging what he had already known. Leonard's confession was simply a retelling of the newspaper story. He had involved the Ricky of his sex fantasies into a fantasy of murder.

Philip struggled to remember exactly what Leonard had said at his last confession. More important was how had he responded.

"Listen to me. I want to help you. You imagine these things. They're fantasies, daydreams."

"No! They are real! Why won't you believe me? I need someone to believe me. No one listens. No one pays attention to me."

Leonard had been desperate to have his shadow life be real. Instead, Philip had tried to yank him into a world he wasn't equipped to handle. Frustrated, Leonard must have obsessed over the newspaper account and gone to the police. If they believed him, it would give his fantasies the validation that his priest had withheld.

Standing up, he noticed a nearly completed crossword puzzle and read the clue for the only word with a missing letter--a regional term for baffled. He took out his pen and added a tidy X.

Flummoxed, the perfect word.

Leaving the store, he held up the fold of newspaper with the article to let Joe know he was taking it. In response, Joe took a red pack out of the case and offered it to him. Philip already had the door open. All he had to do was walk out. He didn't. Pulling a ten dollar bill out of his wallet, he tossed it on the counter and picked up his cigarettes. He didn't look up when he collected his change. This time, Joe's smirk would have bothered him.

At home, he checked his phone messages and heard nothing that required immediate attention. Tossing the cigarettes on the kitchen table, he turned away for a moment, then snatched up the pack and broke the cellophane. After going without cigarettes for so many months, he didn't need to worry that an occasional smoke would revitalize the habit. He lit one, using matches this time, and took a deep drag.

He had never intended to accept Tara's invitation to dinner but hadn't taken time for lunch. Hungry, he found the thought of a plate of lasagna tempting. Tara was easy to talk to. He would be on his guard and never let their friendship go too far. Talking to her would help him get his mind off Leonard.

It struck him that he had mentioned having DVDs for the boys. He wasn't sure which of his DVDs he'd had in mind and stopped to buy a couple he thought the boys would enjoy.

The closest parking space to the DeVeccio house was a block away. He walked the distance at a leisurely pace, no need to dash. It didn't matter if anyone saw him. Nothing was wrong with visiting a parishioner.

"Father! I was afraid you wouldn't make it," were the eager words that greeted him.

"Well, I'm here," he said.

They stared at each other, neither smiling. Catching himself, he said, "I can't wait to dive into a plate of lasagna."

"Yes, of course," she said, seeming flustered. "The boys are watching TV. I'll call them. Dinner will be on the table in a moment."

Looking freshly scrubbed, Derek and David appeared and took their places. The table was already set and adorned with a pair of bright yellow mums in a tall jar. Tara set out the lasagna in a colorful baking dish, then handed Philip a glass of red wine in an ornate, crystal glass.

"Wine with lasagna," he said, "a perfect combination, and this glass is beautiful."

"A wedding present. I should throw it out."

Philip folded his hands, ready to say grace. Before he began Tara said, "Father, if it is all right, Derek will say grace for us."

"Yeah," Derek said. "I had to practice for an hour." He bowed his head, crossed himself, and spieled off a rapid grace.

"I'm sure God was impressed," Philip said, smiling. He took a sip of wine. "Let's see if your mom's cooking tastes as good as it smells."

Philip was pleased that the boys didn't seem the least inhibited by his presence. A priest at the table could dampen the mood, but Tara's boys were as lively as ever. They were terrific boys. Despite being in a tough situation, Tara was doing a good job, but raising them on her own had to be difficult.

After they finished the lasagna and a dessert of spumoni, Tara chased the boys away with the admonition they get going on their homework. She told Philip to stay seated, but he helped her load dishes into the sink, noticing for the first time that a dishwasher wasn't a feature of the tiny kitchen. "You wash. I'll dry," he said.

"No!" She started to protest, then laughed. "Okay, Father. If you want to help, the towels are in that drawer."

They finished quickly, too quickly. It was probably time for him to leave, but he wasn't ready. They talked, an ambling conversation that went nowhere until she said, "I think you have something heavy on your mind. Maybe, I can help."

Her perception startled him. "It'll work out," he said, realizing she wouldn't buy a cheerful assertion that everything was fine.

"Does it," she asked hesitantly, "have anything to do with the murdered man they found in the park? I mean, two men from your parish are involved, and I just wonder..." Her voice trailed off.

He stared at her. Nothing he said, nothing he could have said, should have alerted her, yet somehow she had zoomed in and known or at least suspected. "Why in the world did you ask that?" He sounded brusque, definitely sharper than he intended.

"I'm sorry. I don't know why I asked that. Somehow, it just popped into my head."

Of all the things she might have come up with, she had landed on the right square. It was as if she had read his mind. Unnerved, he needed to collect himself and thought of the cigarettes in his pocket. He hadn't intended to smoke another so soon, but one now couldn't hurt.

Opening the door, he pulled a chair onto the small landing. "I'll blow the smoke out this way," he said, striking a match. "It won't get in the house."

"Father," Tara said, her voice reproachful, "I was so proud of you for quitting."

"I did! I did quit. One now and then doesn't mean anything."

"If you're smoking again, it's because you're worried. Whatever it is, maybe someone can help you."

"If you're thinking of my confessor, it's not a problem that--"

She interrupted. "No, I was thinking of someone professional, like a lawyer or something."

Philip leaned his chair back so far it would have fallen if not for the railing. Slowly, he blew smoke into the night air. "I should have thought of that."

CHAPTER 6

Turning onto Michigan Avenue, Philip braced against a sharp wind. He was on foot, preferring a subway ride to driving downtown and searching for a place to park. He entered the Murray F. Tuley building through the massive glass and metal door. The foyer was several stories high, and a huge chandelier hung from the ceiling. The wide marble stairway had an ornate iron banister, and several women, probably office workers, were ensconced on the lower stairs enjoying brown bag lunches. Philip thought they added a decorative touch to all the gleaming tile and fake gold trim.

He took the elevator to the tenth floor. It had been two, maybe three, years since he had been here, and he had never seen the woman at the reception desk. Her name plate read *Miss Bancroft*, no first name. She sat rigidly erect and had a manikin smile.

"May I help you?"

"I want to talk to Mr. Rockcastle. I didn't phone, but if you tell him I'm here—"

"Mr. Rockcastle is very busy," she said, interrupting in a markedly nasal voice, "If you wish, I may be able to schedule an appointment."

"Please, let Charles know I need to see him." It was warm indoors, and Philip unzipped his jacket.

Miss Bancroft gave him a hard second look. "Father?" she said, making the word a question. She hesitated. "If you tell me your name, perhaps I can let Mr. Rockcastle know you want to see him."

"I'm his brother. If he is busy, I can wait until he has a few minutes."

"Mr. Rockcastle never mentioned that he has a brother who is a priest."

Philip put the palm of his hand on her desk, leaned toward her, and whispered, "I never tell anyone I have a brother who's a lawyer."

Miss Bancroft put her hand on the intercom but, apparently changing her mind, stood up, gave Philip a dubious look, and went into the main office. She left the door slightly ajar and Philip overheard. "Sorry to interrupt, but there is a priest here who says he is your brother." She sounded doubtful.

"Philip," Charles bellowed. "Come in. I'm on a conference call. It won't take long."

He waved him to a chair, but Philip went to the window. Looking down, he could see the broad expanse of Grant Park and beyond it Lake Michigan churning up whitecaps. A tall column of water shot skyward from the Buckingham fountain. Sprays arching from the base of the fountain caught sunlight to create a rainbow mist.

"It's quite a view," he said when Charles finished his call.

"How's the car behaving?"

"Great, I'm enjoying it." Philip picked up a framed picture from a collection on a mahogany side-table. For a brief moment, he allowed himself to imagine, then carefully set the picture down. "Charlene looks grown up."

"I wish she acted grown up. She finished her senior year with straight A's, but she's a daredevil and not afraid of anything. That worries me."

"I can't see her taking any serious risks. She's too smart a girl. Is she settled in at Notre Dame now?"

"After a couple of weeks, she decided it wasn't the right school for her. Last weekend she packed up and drove home. She says next year she wants to enroll at the University of Hawaii and major in surfboarding."

"Really? They offer a surfboarding major?"

"She claims she can get them to start one." He sighed and shook his head. "Eighteen-year-old girls are good for the aspirin industry."

Philip smiled. "Are you calling my niece a headache?"

"Not always. She can be brilliant, but her judgment hasn't caught up to her brain. Raising a teenage girl, you can't imagine..." He broke off. "Sorry."

Philip gave a baffled shrug, but he understood. His brother's apology was unnecessary. Life had unfolded the way it was meant to.

"Phil, I have a hunch you did not come all the way up here to admire the view."

"All the way up," Philip repeated. "You say that as if you think I climbed the stairs. Actually, I knew enough to take the elevator."

Charles laughed. "I'm proud of you, little brother. Now that you're up here, tell me what's wrong."

His showing up without notice made Charles suspicious, and Philip was impressed. His brother could read people and never missed anything, probably why he was such a successful attorney. No point in wasting more time with banter.

"Charles, I need your help."

Charles pointed to the leather chair next to the desk and, leaning back, swiveled his own chair. "Take your time and tell me about it."

Seasoned words, an introduction Charles undoubtedly used with clients. It almost made Philip feel as if he were preparing to make a confession. "Bless me big brother for I have sinned." He blew off the thought.

"Did you hear about the unidentified man found dead in Humboldt Park?"

"I don't think so. What is your interest?"

Philip sucked in his breath. He had to be careful and tell what he knew without reference to Leonard's confession. "The police have classified it as a homicide, and Leonard Wilson, a young man I know from my parish, told the police he was responsible. He implicated another man as his accomplice." Philip was on safe ground. He had said only what had been reported on the news.

"Phil, if you're trying to find someone to defend them, remember I'm a divorce attorney." He made a wide gesture, indicating the luxurious office. Divorce paid well.

"I am not asking you to defend them. Actually, I don't know what I'm asking for, but Charles—-" Leaning forward, Philip grasped the edge of the desk. "I know neither of them had anything to do with the murder."

"Phil, how do you know?" Dropping his voice, he added, "Or is that something you can't talk about?"

"I'm positive. We'll let it go at that." He knew Charles would think he heard someone else confess to the crime, but truth was out of bounds.

Charles swiveled his chair. "If all they have is this man's confession, no corroborating evidence, the case probably won't go far."

"Are you saying innocent people are never convicted?"

"Hell, no. If everyone wrongly convicted walked free, some prisons could be rented out as no-star hotels. But cases are dropped when a district attorney doesn't have enough evidence to prosecute."

"I'm afraid Leonard's confession might hold up."

"Why would this man confess if he wasn't involved?"

"It's complicated." It was the best answer Philip could give.

Standing up, Charles went to the window. With his back to Philip, he shook his head. "What makes you think I can do anything?"

Philip didn't have an answer, only memories of his brother coaxing him through that black time. "The only two places I could think of to go for help are you and God."

Charles sat down again. "You put me in good company, but God is your better bet."

"Always," Philip said, getting ready to leave.

Charles held up his hand. "Not so fast."

The intercom sounded, and Charles touched the key. "Persy, apologize for me. Say I'll be a while longer.

"Persy? Is that Miss Bancroft's name?"

Charles nodded. "Persimmon."

Hardly a moment to be amused, but Philip suspected he knew why the name was not displayed.

"We would have a better idea of what to do if we knew what evidence the police have," Charles said. "Do these guys have a lawyer?"

"They can't afford one."

"A public defender will get the case." Charles flipped through his speed dial index. "Jerry Finlay is a private investigator I use to do a little surveillance, mostly checking on wayward spouses or spouses we hope to catch being wayward. He's a retired cop and still has contacts in the PD."

"And you think he can help us?"

"He can probably find out how good a case the police have against these two. What are their names?"

"Leonard Wilson and Fedrico Haldero. Fedrico goes by Ricky."

"Do you know if they have criminal records? Finlay should check that first."

"I don't think Leonard does."

"What do you know about him?"

"On the news, they gave his age as twenty-five. I took him for younger. He lives with his mother. I think the only job he ever had was working summers at the concession in the park. He wanders around, helping carry groceries or shoveling snow for neighbors—-that sort of thing. It's made him something of a neighborhood pet."

"The other one—-Haldero. Does he have a record?"

"According to his mother, just relatively small stuff. Smoking pot once. When he was fourteen, he took a car for a joy ride. She said no assaults, nothing violent."

"If he has an alibi, it might shoot down the whole confession. Do you know if he has one that will stand up?"

Philip shook his head. "Not according to my deacon. Don appointed himself parish watchdog. I don't know where he picked up the information, but last night he gave me a call and said Haldero doesn't have an alibi. When the police picked him up, he thought it was because he bought a bag from the neighborhood entrepreneur that night. He lied and said he had been with his girl friend. When she knew a murder was involved, she bowed out and said she hadn't even talked to him."

"Phil, I don't know if Finlay can help us, but let's give it a try."

"What's the tab for detective work?"

"Probably more than you can pay, so leave it with me. But you have to do something."

"What's that?"

"You haven't done anything wrong. Promise me you won't kick yourself black and blue if we can't help these guys."

His brother was right as usual. Philip had not done anything wrong. Why couldn't he shake the feeling that Leonard Wilson's murder confession was his fault?

CHAPTER 7

Charles watched Philip leave but first he made him promise to come out to the house soon. "It's been a long time, and Charlene can brief you on her plans to sponsor a major in surf boarding."

They had both laughed, putting an upbeat finish on their conference, but Charles was uneasy. Philip's worry about the murder went deep--too deep if he knew his kid brother. After swearing off cigarettes, he was smoking again, not enough to reek of it, but enough for Charles to have caught the aroma. He had a hunch Philip was lighting up because of his involvement or, more likely, perceived involvement in a crime.

Charles glanced at his appointment schedule then touched the intercom. "Persy, is Mrs. Bailer waiting?"

"She's been here for twenty minutes and is getting restless."

"Tell her it will be a while longer. And, Persy, when my brother shows up, I always have time to see him."

With the fees he charged, his clients didn't expect to be kept waiting, but he was confident Mrs. Bailer would forget her annoyance when he showed her the set of eight by ten glossies in her file. On her behest, he had hired Jerry Finlay to find out if her husband was involved with another woman. Charles could report her suspicions had been half right. Her husband was involved, but the other woman was a man.

This was not the first time sleuthing for one of his clients had revealed an unexpected gender for the liaison. To Charles' surprise, when he told one woman her competition was male, instead of being distressed, she was jubilant. "I couldn't stand losing him to another woman, but a man! Nothing I can do about that."

This assignment for Jerry Finlay was different. He dialed the number and, before the third ring, heard Jerry's growl of a voice. The detective didn't have an office. The address he claimed was in a run-down section of the city where stately mansions of old had been converted into rooming houses at best and God knows what at worst. Finlay had told Charles his favorite assignments were the ones where they nailed the wife, claiming his own three divorces had left him holding empty candy wrappers.

"Jerry, I have a job for you," Charles told him, "but not a divorce this time. Do you think you can get information about two men being held as murder suspects?"

"Are you defending them?"

"That's hardly my line."

"So what's your interest?"

Charles hesitated, not sure whether he should mention Philip, but he had to provide Jerry with some groundwork. "Someone is concerned about the strength of the case against them."

"These two guys--what are their names?"

Charles looked at his notepad. "Leonard Wilson and Fedrico Haldero. I think he said Fedrico goes by Ricky."

"Who is this *he* you're talking about?"

Charles thought it over. "My brother."

"The one you said was a priest?" His tone made it a question.

"My only brother. He believes these two are innocent. He's hoping the case against them won't hold up."

"What do we know so far?"

Charles shrugged. "Not much." He repeated what Philip had told him. "Jerry, probably the place to start checking would be the local police in the area."

Charles heard a deep-throated chuckle. "You're catching on. If you get tired of listening to rich broads complain about husbands enjoying a little sex on the side, maybe you can start a detective career as my assistant. Lower pay scale than you're used to."

Charles was accustomed to what Jerry probably thought of as humor. He knew better than to inquire about his methods. If he ever skipped around the law when getting his evidence, Charles was adamant about not wanting to know, but legality was never a threat. A man photographed having a pleasant encounter with his secretary at a discreet motel was not likely to bring a suit for invasion of privacy and display the photos as evidence.

With this assignment, Charles didn't expect photographs. The best Jerry could do was report that the case against Wilson and Haldero appeared too weak to take to court.

"Jerry, I haven't told you much, but I hope you can get somewhere with it."

"Well, Chuck," Jerry said, using a nickname Charles detested, "checking out the dead guy has to be the place to start. I take it the rates will be the same, expenses plus hours."

Charles agreed, then added, "Get back to me right away if you come up with anything worthwhile. I hope I can let him know something encouraging." This time he didn't have to identify the *him* involved.

CHAPTER 8

Philip looked forward to spending an hour or two at Octoberfest, still held in the area of the city where the greeting on the streets had once been "Wie geht's?" Although much of the German population had moved on, their annual celebration endured. Knockwurst with sauerkraut was sold at makeshift booths and eaten outdoors on picnic benches or umbrella sheltered tables. An accordionist occasionally strolled the scene, playing old German tunes.

Tara had told him she was going to be there on Friday, helping a friend in one of the booths. Philip admitted the likelihood of seeing her was a greater attraction than washing down heavy German cooking with a stein of beer. So what if they ran into each other? The most they would do was talk, possibly sit together at a table, always in innocent view of dozens of people.

He started to put on his black suit coat, then decided it would be too warm and opted for a light blue cardigan. His collar still showed.

While he was locking the rectory door, an elderly woman rushed toward him. She was bent and frail, tears streaked her face. "Father, I must ask you. There is something I have to know." She sobbed out the words.

"Mrs. Tarber," he said, recognizing the face behind the tears. He put his arm around her and led her inside. When they were seated, he waited. She would talk when she composed herself.

"Rupert." Still fighting sobs, she gasped the name. "I found him dead this morning. I don't know how I'll get along without him."

"I am very sorry," Philip said, sharing her pain. "Let us ask God to give you strength as He accepts your husband into His kingdom."

"My husband?" Looking up from a sodden handkerchief, she said, "Jack died ten years ago."

"Who was dear Rupert?"

"Rupert was my Chihuahua. That's why I'm here. I have to be sure I will see him again. Dogs, I mean good dogs, go to heaven, don't they, Father?"

The church's position was clear. Animals were deemed not to have souls, and only souls were eternal. Philip didn't want to tell this woebegone woman she could not look forward to a reunion with her pet. Instead, he said, "You and Rupert loved each other, and love never dies. More important," he added gently, "you can look forward to seeing your husband in heaven and--"

She interrupted. "Him?" she looked annoyed and gave an airy wave of her hand. "I won't waste time in heaven looking for Jack. He'll need help if he looks for me. Never could do anything on his own."

Philip cleared his throat.

For the next fifteen minutes, he listened to accounts of Rupert's marvelous ways, then he recited a prayer, asking God to comfort her in her sorrow. Standing up, Philip said, "I'm sure Rupert would want you to give a sad, lonely, little dog a good home and someone to love."

"Yes...yes he would," she said, brightening. "Father, you've been such a comfort."

At his second try, Philip got clear of the door and made it to his car. The festival was well-attended, and he had to park a distance away. Walking passed the barricade closing the street to through traffic, he heard someone call.

"Father Rockcastle."

Tara moved out of the shadow of a catalpa tree clinging to the last of its leaves. Her deep red blouse accented the dark hair that hung loose to her shoulders. He caught a glint of silver earrings.

"Good evening, Mrs. DeVeccio."

A woman from his parish hurried up. "Father, we have room at our table. Please join us. You can tell Mike what you want to eat. He'll get it for you."

Smiling, he edged away from her. "Thank you, but I'm going to walk around a bit."

Tara caught his eye. Her glance told him to go across the street. He did and strolled passed several food booths, greeting people and stopping to buy beer served in a tall, paper cup. He wasn't sure where to go until he realized Tara had managed to get ahead of him. She stopped at a table where a young woman was seated.

"Father Rockcastle!" Tara called, sounding more surprised than she had minutes earlier. "Come and meet a friend of mine."

Tara made the introduction. With the music and general din, Philip didn't catch the woman's name. "Nice to meet you, Father," she said, her voice a bit singsong as she glanced from Tara to him. "Tara helped me serve sauerkraut. I have to go scrub the smell off my hands." She gave them another look and blended into the crowd.

Philip and Tara sat down at the tiny, round table that wobbled badly, either from uneven legs or uneven pavement. When Philip set his beer down, Tara cautioned him to hold on to it. "This table shakes. It could spill."

For several minutes, they talked about the table, agreeing that it was old and the metal construction had probably long been rusted. Tara said she was glad it hadn't rained and spoiled the evening. Philip agreed and added his own mindless comments about the pleasant weather.

They had always fallen into conversation easily. Now they acted unexpectedly self-conscious. Philip was baffled until it occurred to him that never before had they seen each other away from their respective places. This encounter was different. Each knew the other would be there. Without actually saying the words, they had agreed to meet. What they were experiencing was reminiscent of the awkwardness of a first date, but it was not a date. He would not allow it to be a date.

"Where are the boys?" he asked.

"Nothing here would interest them, so I let them visit their grandmother." After another silence, she said, "I thought you would be here earlier."

"I was delayed."

The cold beer was refreshing. He drained the cup and crushed it in his hand. Suddenly, he grinned. "Actually, I was delayed by a dead Chihuahua."

Despite the genuine compassion he felt for Mrs. Tarber, he couldn't deny the humor in her devotion to a dog and indifference to a husband. Never mentioning Mrs. Tarber's name, he told Tara how indignant she had acted when he mistakenly thought her grief was for her husband.

Philip had never seen Tara laugh so hard. He noticed how she tipped her head back and closed her eyes. It might have been wrong for him to amuse her with a story about a parishioner, but it didn't feel wrong. The self-consciousness was gone. He could tell her anything.

"Father, you were right to tell the woman to get another dog." A shadow fell across her face. In a sarcastic tone she added, "Her husband couldn't have been too bad or she wouldn't think he was in heaven."

"Are you still in love with him?" The question jumped out.

"Not anymore. I was in love with him, but my marriage was a disaster."

"I'm sorry."

They were silent again, but now it soothed.

When she spoke, she sounded wistful. "Did you always want to be a priest?"

"Since I was in fifth grade."

A vivid memory flashed of the day when he had listened to Sister Mary Agnes tell about the joy of dedicating your life to God. "Many are called," she had said, "but only the blessed few are chosen."

He had sat up straight, folded his hands atop his desk and prayed, "Please, Lord, choose me."

God had chosen him. He was certain of it. It had not been a direct path, but he was where he belonged, doing what he was meant to do. Looking at Tara, he caught his breath. Nothing, no one, could be allowed to change that.

"I don't suppose...I mean, it isn't a good question to ask a priest, but..."

"But what?"

"Philip," she said softly, saying his name for the first time, "were you ever in love?"

"Yes."

"What happened?" Seeming to catch herself, she said, "I'm sorry. I shouldn't have asked."

"I don't mind. It was a long time ago, and I wasn't a priest."

"Did you give her up for the priesthood?"

Philip had never thought of it that way, but it was true. "Yes," he said, "I gave her up for the priesthood." Another memory flooded and with it a familiar sense of loneliness. No one had ever eased it, not until now, but this could not continue. He was on the edge of a precipice. If this was their first date, he had to make certain it was also their last.

In the final moments he would ever share with her this way, he could be honest with himself. He wanted to hold her, love her, protect her. He wanted to help her raise her sons. Slowly, he lifted the hand she rested atop the table and ran his index finger along the lines on her palm.

"Do you read palms?"

"No," he said, "but I can read yours."

"What does it say?"

"It says someone who cares very much about you has to say goodbye."

CHAPTER 9

After he left the festival, Philip drove through the park, pulling off on a secluded section of road sheltered by trees. Rolling the window down, he reached for his cigarettes. He needed one--maybe two or three--it didn't matter.

This was not the first time he'd had to say goodbye. Memories were stoked. If only they could fade like the smoke he exhaled into the night, but they lingered, vivid and haunting.

He told Tara about the first time he had felt the call. The thought had consumed him, and he had continued to pray. After finishing eighth grade, he entered preparatory seminary. During the next four years, he was confident his prayers had been answered; he was, indeed, called to the priesthood. At eighteen, he left home for the seminary. Three years later, ordination loomed. It would soon be time to receive First Orders.

When he was home for a few weeks summer respite, several old friends drove over and tried to talk him into joining them for a day at the beach. Without being told, he knew the agenda-— girl gathering forays and plenty of beer guzzling from innocently disguised containers. That was not for him. He wasn't swayed by arguments that he deserved more fun than he could get at the seminary.

He did squeeze into the car and ride part way to the beach. Then he split and walked a distance to the main library. He roamed through book stacks, selected a couple of interesting titles, and took them to a table near a window.

"God damn!"

Those were the first words he heard her say. He must have looked disapproving because, glancing across the table at him, she said, "Whoops! I'm sorry."

"If you have a problem, perhaps I can assist you." He was going to be a priest. It wasn't too early to practice counseling.

"My problem is stupidity."

"Don't be too hard on yourself," he said gravely. "I'm sure everyone feels stupid occasionally."

"I didn't think I held the patent," she said, giving him an exasperated look. She brushed back a lock of hair, He was struck by the unusual color.

"Your hair," he said, "what color do you call it?"

She shrugged. "Reddish-brown, I guess. Someone called it mahogany."

"Mahogany--that's a good name for it. But your stupidity," he added, wondering why he had noticed her hair, "How did it manifest this time?"

"This time?" she repeated, raising her eyebrows until they disappeared behind her bangs. "This time, if you must know, I forgot to bring the list of topics I'm supposed to be researching." She pushed back from the table.

"Perhaps, you can call home and have someone read the list to you."

"My mom's the only one there, and she can never read my writing. Anyway, if it's not here," she said, indicating an open notebook, "I don't know where it is."

She thrust her lower lip forward in a comical pout. Philip never indulged in teasing, but something about that pout inspired him. "Even without the patent, you do have a problem with stupidity," he said. "Perhaps, you should take vitamins."

"Vitamins for stupidity? That's a new one."

"Vitamin B for brains. Maybe, a large dose will help."

She leaned toward him, her expression suddenly serene. "Do you take Vitamin B for brains?"

"Of course," he said, trying to sound serious.

"Ha!" she roared, "it's a shame they don't work."

She was clearly pleased with her retort and soon they were trading silly barbs and laughing.

Philip had been around girls before, including several whose amorous advances seemed determined to undermine his commitment to celibacy. This girl wasn't trying to entice him. They were just having fun—-too much fun. A librarian hushed them.

"You two must be quiet or you'll have to leave."

"I'm sorry," Philip said.

The girl giggled. "See what you've done?"

Philip stood up. "Of course," he said. "I sat here talking and laughing all by myself. Come on. Let's go."

They left the library and walked east to Grant Park. When they approached a street vendor, Philip offered to buy her a hot dog.

"Okay," she said, "you buy me one. I'll buy me one. Then I'll have two."

"Right. And I'll buy one for me, and you'll buy one for me. Then I'll have two." They were talking nonsense, but talking nonsense and laughing felt strange and refreshing, like realizing you had been cold when suddenly smothered in sunlight.

When they got their hot dogs, the girl took out her wallet. Philip pushed her hand away. "My good deed for getting you kicked out of the library."

"We weren't kicked out."

"No, but it was coming. I couldn't stop laughing at you."

Ignoring benches, they ate the hot dogs while strolling through the park. They managed to talk between bites, and everything she said struck Philip as funny. It must have worked two ways, because she was laughing, too.

Later, he walked her to the subway station and was watching her go down the stairs when he thought of something. "Hey," he shouted. "What's your name?"

"Susanna," she called, glancing back.

"Will you be at the library tomorrow?"

People hurried around her, but he caught her words. "No, but maybe on Friday."

Maybe. It was not much to go on, but he couldn't remember ever laughing so much. It would be fun to see her again. He didn't think of it as a date with a girl.

On Friday, he returned to the library, snatched up a book, and sat down at their table. He made a stab at reading, but kept glancing at his watch. "One hour," he told himself. "If she's not here by then--"

"Hi."

"Susanna." He said her name for the first time.

"I suppose you have a name."

"Phil Rockcastle," he said, surprising himself. He always called himself Philip, never Phil.

She had her list of topics, and he helped her put together a bibliography. Sitting by her side, he couldn't help noticing her profile and the way her chin thrust forward when she concentrated.

Suddenly, she gathered up her books. "That's enough. Let's see if the hotdog man is still in business."

The vendor was ensconced in his usual spot. They bought their hot dogs, then walked to the Art Institute.

"I wish I had my camera," Susanna said. "I'd make you climb up on a lion and pose for a picture."

"Stone lion climbing is forbidden. You're still trying to get me in trouble."

They were adept at making each other laugh, whether at something or nothing. It seemed natural to agree to see her the next day, but he never forgot he was almost a priest. Their outings were to public places, and he never touched her.

She said fish fascinated her, and they spent a whole afternoon at the Shedd Aquarium. He had only a short time left at home and spending it with Susanna was vitalizing. She had a vibrancy that put him in touch with something in himself he hadn't known existed.

They did manage a few serious conversations. One touched on religion, and both said they were Catholic. That was when he should have told her. He didn't.

When he said his vacation was over and he was going away, she asked for his picture. "Something to throw darts at when I feel stupid," she said. They were in a Starbucks, drinking lattes and waiting for the rain to let up. She laid her hand on top of his. In a much softer voice she said, "A picture to show my girlfriends and look at once in a while."

The next evening, he borrowed his brother's convertible. He picked her up where they had agreed to meet and took her for a leisurely ride down Outer Drive. With the top down, a brisk wind blew in their faces. This was their first outing in a car, and something was different. There was none of the usual banter, just a quiet sense of companionship. He hadn't known where she lived but, following her directions, he drove her home and parked in front of her house. After a long, awkward silence, she turned toward him and was moving closer, seeming ready for an embrace. Pulling back, he handed her a photo.

"I can't see it," she said.

He switched on the interior light.

"Phil, that's you. What are you wearing?"

"My cassock. I'm studying to be a priest. I'll be ordained next year."

He had decided it would be all right to give her a friendly kiss goodbye, but never got the chance. She opened the car door, tossed the picture at him, and said, "If I ever get married, you can perform the ceremony." She gave him one, final look before bolting from the car with a moaned, "Oh, Phil."

"*Oh, Phil,*" The sound of her voice, the look on her face, had stayed with him a long time. It still reached out.

He ground out his cigarette. There was no dilemma. Susanna belonged to the past. Tara belonged to a future that could never be.

CHAPTER 10

Philip was changing his clothes after Tuesday morning Mass when the doorbell rang. Before he could answer, there was violent knocking. Someone had to be pounding hard with both hands. He shoved his arms into the sleeves of his shirt.

"Okay," he shouted, "I'm coming."

He slid back the cover on the door's security window. The person was either desperate or angry, and he had to know what to expect. When he recognized the contorted face, he yanked the door open.

"Father, help us. Please help us. They let Rico phone home. He says tomorrow they take him to court. He has to make a plea--say if he did it, say if he killed someone. This public defender woman wants him to say he is guilty, that he did some kind of slaughter. Manslaughter, maybe. She says all they will give him is twenty years. That's not giving," she sobbed. "That's taking."

"Mrs. Garcia, please come in my office and sit down. We can talk and--"

"No, no. I don't want to sit down. Talking won't help my Rico. I want you to do something. My Rico, he said you believed him--believed he didn't kill nobody. And you do. You do believe it." Her words gushed. Her eyes were ringed and swollen. She had the dignity of her heritage and would never give way to convulsive tears for anything less vital.

He took her arm. "Come and sit down. I insist."

She resisted, repeating, "You do believe him. You believe he didn't do what they say."

The answer to Philip's quick, desperate prayer did not arrive. He didn't know what to do. Focusing on the floor, he said, "Based on what little I know about the case, I can't--" He broke off, raised his head, and met her gaze. "Yes, Senora, I believe your son is innocent."

"You help him. Please, Father, help him."

This time she didn't resist when led her into his office. "I don't know if I can, but I promise to try."

Sitting down, she went limp, the aggression gone that had pounded on the door. More in Spanish than English, she said she was sorry for bringing him trouble. "But I had to. What else? What else?"

"Don't apologize," he said. "Senora, I have already done something that might help us." Saying *us* was deliberate. She needed the comfort of thinking she was not alone.

"I have to warn you this might come to nothing, but I talked to a lawyer. He won't charge us and--"

She interrupted. "This lawyer friend, will he defend Rico? He thinks the public defender woman don't care if he's not the right guy. She wants it over quick, but not over for him for twenty years."

"This lawyer only handles divorce cases. He hired a detective to help us find out exactly what evidence the police have against Rico."

"All they got is that loco guy telling them loco things," she said, anger flooding her voice. "Believe me, Father, that is all they got. Just Lenny loco."

This was almost a replay of Philip's first meeting with her, but not quite. At their earlier meeting, he had promised to visit Rico. Now, he realized the person he had to visit was Lenny loco. He didn't share that with her. Instead, he said, "I will do everything I can to assist your son."

He thought he sounded too formal, but the words touched her. Clasping her hands together, she smiled. "Father, I know you will assist; you will help. You work for God. God will show you how to help my Rico."

She left comforted by new hope and calmer than when she came. For Philip, it was another matter. She wasn't just trusting him to help Rico. She was trusting God through him. It was Philip's responsibility to make certain God did not let her down.

He knew he should take the situation to his superiors but rejected the thought, knowing what his bishop--what anyone in authority--would say:

Pray and stay out of it.

Wise advice, but it would be too late. In his heart, he was already in it and had to visit Leonard before his court date. He made several phone calls rescheduling the day's appointments and, certain that Leonard would have already been transferred, left for the county jail. Driving south across the city, Philip didn't mind the lagging traffic. It gave him a chance to consider the best approach.

He hoped a few days in the lock-up had jarred Leonard into some semblance of judgment. The pathetic young man had to realize he had created a fantasy that couldn't be resolved by promising to say a few Hail Marys. Leonard would recant his confession. When he did, Philip could provide evidence showing he had made arrangements for Leonard to go to a mental health clinic. That would at least show that Leonard's parish priest thought he was mentally disturbed.

Philip was almost certain Leonard would be ready to admit his total knowledge of the murder was gleaned from the newspaper. Unfortunately, his first glimpse of Leonard dashed any hope.

Philip was in a visiting room, seated on one side of a glass partition. Leonard was led in wearing jailhouse issue and a delighted smile. "Father Rockcastle, how kind of you to pay me a visit." He acted like someone greeting an unexpected guest. Sitting down, he folded his hands in front of him and gave his head an arrogant tilt.

Philip had expected contrition or at least a realistic dose of anxiety. Taken back by Leonard's aplomb, he didn't know where to begin. Leonard spared him a decision. "Father, I want you to hear my confession. It will be quite interesting. I committed a murder."

Quite interesting. I committed a murder.

This man was psychotic, far more deranged than Philip had suspected. It stabbed him to realize his efforts to help Leonard had been at best futile and at worst dangerous. If Leonard wanted the Sacrament of Penance now, he had to contact another priest. "Leonard, I'm not hear to listen to your confession. I'm here because I want to help you, and I want to help Ricky."

"It will help me to make a confession. You can hear Ricky's confession too, but you have to hear me first. I killed someone."

"Leonard, all you know about a murder is what you read in the newspaper. Think hard. Isn't that where you found out about it?" He was backing Leonard into a corner and regretted the words even as he said them.

"No! The police talk to me every day. Detectives talk to me, too. They ask me questions. At first I didn't know about the gun. Now I remember, and they believe me."

"A gun?" Philip thought a moment. No gun was mentioned in the newspaper article.

Leonard explained that the first time he was asked about a gun, he couldn't remember it. "Detective Pearson insisted I was holding back, and he was right. I did know about the gun. I had to know about it. They asked if it was Ricky's gun. They kept asking and finally I told them the truth. We used Ricky's gun.

"They asked me how we got him into the recreation center." Smiling, he said, "That was easy. I worked in the park and knew you could get into the center from downstairs by the boat dock. That's how we did it. We were careful and no one saw us."

Philip visualized the recreation center. A lower section of the building bordered the lagoon and did not have an exterior wall, creating a sheltered dock under the main floor for row boats. Transporting anything bulky over the narrow walkway between the water and the dock would be difficult. Transporting a dead body seemed impossible.

Philip leaned forward, "Leonard, pay attention! You couldn't have gotten him inside that way."

Leonard hesitated. "I had a hard time remembering how we got him to the supply room. Detective McVoy--he likes me--asked if we used a carpet or something to drag him on. That was exactly how we did it. There were things I couldn't remember, but he helped me. Now, I remember all of it."

Philip slumped back in his chair. He wanted to believe it was accidental, but accidental or deliberate, the police were feeding Leonard information. Leonard regularly convinced himself he was a participant in sexual activities he read about. He would have no trouble putting himself into any picture the police described to him.

"Listen! This is terribly serious. Leonard, you had no reason to kill anyone. You have to think about it--"

"No! I remember exactly, everything that they told me. I did have a reason to kill him. Ricky needed money for drugs so he had to rob someone. Ricky's my friend. I had to help him. That's the truth, I know it for sure."

Philip couldn't keep the exasperation out of his voice. "Before you talked to the police, you didn't even know the man's name."

"You never believed me when I told you about me and Ricky, but the police believe me." Leonard held his head high and looked smug. "They believe we killed a man. They didn't know his name at first, but now they do. It was Barton Corbin. Isn't that a nice name?"

Philip slumped in his chair.

CHAPTER 11

Jerry Finlay waited for three-day old bread to toast, then dipped it into his instant coffee. He usually downed a bacon and eggs breakfast at a neighborhood cafe and for dessert enjoyed a little sexy banter with the more than rotund owner. He once asked what measured more, her waist or her height. Far from being offended, Tessa had succumbed to girlish giggles. Exchanges with her were sometimes as close to socializing as he would get for the day. This morning, he didn't have time for Tessa.

The assignment puzzled him. Rockcastle could contact the public defender and eventually get whatever evidence the prosecution had surrendered, but the usually cool attorney had been impatient. Jerry suspected it was because his brother was involved, not that the reason mattered. When a client as profitable as Rockcastle needed information, he could oblige. Getting a good read on how strong a case the DA had against murder suspects would require a different approach but was nothing he couldn't handle.

For a moment, Finlay let himself wonder--*a Catholic priest with an interest in a murder*--then he cut off the thought. No point wasting time being curious.

He had never been a gung-ho cop, but he did his job well and had risen to lead detective. Most of his private life was spent flitting in and out of matrimony and planning exotic vacations he never took. Not until he retired did he realize how necessary working had always been to him. His retirement lasted until he couldn't stand the boredom and began a new vocation as a private investigator.

Pippa bit his ankle. The Siamese cat, his only live-in companion, was a squawker with the annoying habit of using her teeth to let him know she wanted to be fed. He shouldn't have named her after an ex-wife. "Okay," he muttered, emptying a can of Friskies into her bowl.

Yesterday, he had checked at the station where Wilson and Haldero had been taken after their arrest. The captain had been willing to share information with a former cop, but he didn't have much that hadn't been made public. Two kids had discovered a body. There was no wallet or driver's license, and identification had been made through fingerprints. The dead man was Barton Corbin. He had served a short stint in prison for illegal practices as a real estate manager. He'd had other minor run-ins with the law but nothing recent.

A few days after the body was found, Leonard Wilson had marched into the station and confessed to the murder. He named Haldero as his accomplice. One of the boys who had discovered the body in a storage room remembered two guys running from that direction. His description was too foggy to be of use, but it backed up Wilson's story that he was one of a pair. Jerry was on his way to court to witness the pair being arraigned.

It was the first time he had been to the county courthouse since he retired. He hadn't missed it, and he certainly hadn't missed the jail next door. Just being close made him remember a stench that could linger in your nostrils for hours.

The courthouse itself was old, and a wide expanse of concrete steps led to the entrance. The main hall was spacious and crowded with attorneys, defendants, and the typical motley crowd. The rumble of voices indicated most had something to say.

Jerry took the elevator to the third floor where Wilson and Haldero were being arraigned in Judge Torrey Laurence's courtroom. He chose a seat in a back corner with a good view of the room. Not sure of what he was looking for, he needed to see everything.

A man strolled in, hands in pockets, and looked around. The only notable thing about his appearance was a thick mop of white hair. He started toward the seat next to Jerry, then seemed to change his mind and sat down several rows behind a priest.

Jerry hardly needed the Roman collar to identify Rockcastle's brother. The resemblance was unmistakable. Chuck's dark hair was flecked with silver, a suitable touch for a man enthroned behind a highly polished desk in a high-rise office. The priest's hair was one-tone black, thick, and he had a good barber. Jerry's savvy decided that if Father Rockcastle stepped around his vow of chastity, it would be with women. His good looks and general demeanor were definitely masculine. He wouldn't fancy the guys.

The Wilson and Haldero arraignment was the third case on the docket. The first was a domestic violence case, and the complainant was dropping the charges. That should have been the end of it, but Judge Laurence put his oar in with fatherly advice about how the couple should learn to get along for the sake of their children and recommended family counseling.

The second case was more interesting or at least better to look at. A tall brunette who managed to look sexy even in prison issue was charged with the theft of the expensive necklace she had been examining in an upscale jewelry store where she had posed as a prospective buyer. A trial date was set and it was over. No fatherly advice for her.

Wilson and Haldero were brought in. A Mexican woman seated next to Rockcastle's brother leaned forward and raised a hand, more quick acknowledgement than a wave. One of the defendants gave her a lingering look, surely an exchange between mother and son.

The second man was blond and ebullient. Jerry had never seen a prisoner look so thrilled to stand before a judge. Although not fat, he had the fleshiness that goes with lack of exercise. His fair complexion looked as if, in or out of jail, he didn't get much sun. His case was called first: *Leonard Wilson.*

The charges were read, and Wilson's lawyer assured the judge that her client understood. Judge Laurence asked for a plea.

"I'm guilty, your honor. Ricky and I killed that man. We killed Barton Corbin."

"You're crazy! Loco!" Fedrico Haldero tried to lunge toward him, his face tensing into dark red fury. A bailiff moved to stand next to him. The judge gave a sharp warning.

Haldero's plea was loud and vehement "Not guilty! I didn't do it. Judge, I didn't kill nobody. Lenny is crazy."

"Your honor," his counsel said, "I have explained the charges to Mr. Haldero. He understands, and he is aware of the prosecution's offer." Her tone was almost a bored sigh. She did not approve her client's plea.

A tentative trial date was set, and it was over. Leaving the courtroom, Jerry didn't try to intercept Rockcastle's brother. The priest was with Haldero's mother. Any conversation would, at best, be limited, and Jerry had something more pressing on his mind. He was hungry. A piece of toast couldn't see him through the rest of the afternoon, and he remembered that the cafeteria across the street had good food.

The lunch time crowd had already spilled out from the courthouse. At the cafeteria, he had to stand in a long line behind a woman wearing a fur coat that looked as if the original owner might have been killed in a fight. The scruffy fur he recognized from the arraignment, but he hadn't been seated where he could catch the woman's reactions. He was curious. Did she know one of the defendants or had she known Barton Corbin?

He loaded his tray with a bowl of chili and a cheese sandwich. At the urns, he filled a cup of coffee and reached the cash register before the woman paid. "Let me get this," he said.

"Why?" she asked, looking him over.

"We were at the same arraignment. Thought you might want to talk."

She shrugged and picked up her tray. He followed her to a table. So far, the only insight he'd gained from court was that Wilson was either play-acting for an insanity defense or Haldero's cry of loco was right on, not that loco meant innocent. Anyway, her lunch would go on Chuck's tab.

Taking a good look at her, he decided she was probably late thirties, maybe early forties, although an ample application of cosmetics made it hard to be sure. He ate some chili before asking, "What was your interest in court?"

"I loved him." She put her folk down and stared at her plate. "We were together for four years."

"Barton Corbin?" It was a question but, looking at her face, he knew the answer. Before taking another bite, he managed, "I'm sorry. His death must have been a shock. How are you doing?"

She did a quick shift from regret to anger. "I'm pissed. Really pissed."

"It's hard to lose someone, especially that way," Jerry said.

"He's not all I lost." She jerked her head up, and dangling gold earrings bobbed. "He said he had an annuity coming. It sounded like a lot of money, and we talked about going to Hawaii or maybe the Caribbean."

She told him her name was Joyce Cole. The different last name suggested that she and Corbin weren't married, and Jerry asked if she knew who would inherit the annuity.

She shook her head, putting the earrings in motion again. "I don't know. I didn't know anything about the annuity until just a few days before he got killed. He was watching TV--I think a news channel--and something really got to him. He was excited and said there was a good chance a big payout was coming his way, probably with even better payments in the future. He laughed and said he was about to inherit a lifetime annuity."

"Joyce," Jerry asked, deciding with her he could be on an instant first name basis, "Do you know what it was on TV that excited him?"

"It was just something on the news. Some guy was mentioned for something."

"Who was the guy?"

He waited while she took another spoonful of tortilla soup.

"I don't know. I wasn't paying attention, but..." She broke off abruptly and gave him a hard look. "Are you a cop?"

"Joyce, I used to be. I do private detective work now." If you didn't make a habit of it, it didn't hurt to tell the truth.

"If you're a detective, maybe you can help me find out about the annuity. Even with Bart gone, someone should get it."

Her story was getting more interesting than the rest of his sandwich. What on TV could have reminded Corbin of an annuity? It had to have been information about someone he knew. Perhaps, an old friend or acquaintance had won the lottery or made a fortune, and Corbin intended to collect on an unpaid debt. It was possible, but when his detective's mind clicked into action, it came up with extortion.

CHAPTER 12

Leaving the courtroom, Philip took Lydia Garcia's arm. "Let me drive you home."

She said something, English or Spanish, he couldn't tell. It was more moan than words.

In the car, Philip made no attempt at conversation. She was suffering. Only prayer could offer comfort. He prayed aloud, expressing confidence that God would protect Rico from wrongful conviction. Perhaps, she would have more faith in his words than he did.

When they reached her neighborhood, she pointed the way to her house, a two-story bungalow with a ubiquitous tree-of-heaven on the front lawn. It was the same type house the DeVeccios lived in. For a moment, Tara's face loomed up, but he drove her out of mind, refusing to rekindle a fire that had never burned.

Philip started to get out of the car to assist her but she grasped his arm. "Gracias, Father," she said, opening the door herself. "You try to help people."

She was right. He did try to help people, maybe too much. Any doubt about his influence had vanished in the courtroom when Leonard made eye contact with him, then grinned and stretched tall in triumph. His manner conveyed the message. *So what* if *Father Rockcastle didn't believe me; the police do.*

Before going home, Philip ran a few errands. He had just returned to the rectory when he heard a knock accompanied by voices. He glanced at his watch. It was four o'clock, time for a meeting with a committee planning a Christmas sale in the church basement. The sale had hardly been his idea, but he could not refuse people who wanted to raise money to assist needy families in the parish.

When he opened the door, four women traipsed to his office, all eager to tell him their plans.

"Father, we expect to raise at least two hundred dollars and--"

"Two hundred! Matilda, we'll raise at least a thousand."

"Both of you are wrong."

They managed to desist from bickering long enough to outline their plans. At the first lull, Philip said, "I can see that you ladies have everything under control. I appreciate your keeping me informed." He stood up, inviting their departure.

He was warming up the remains of a beef stew a day or two past its prime and deciding whether to open a beer when he heard someone at the door. He was not in the mood to welcome anyone, especially not the man who stood, hands on hips, in the doorway.

"I came early, because I need to talk to you."

"Early? What do you..." Before he finished, Philip realized. This was Wednesday. He had never forgotten his class before, but the scene at the courthouse had distracted him. He was tired. The discouraging day couldn't end soon enough, but he had to hold class.

"We have to talk. It's very important."

Philip groaned inwardly, hardly in the mood for one of Nick's challenges. He had come early and had to think he had a dandy.

"Nick, if you want to attend the class, go in and wait for the others," Philip said sharply. Heading into the kitchen, he ignored the stew and took out a cigarette. It seemed pointless to keep telling himself he only smoked occasionally. He was smoking regularly but assured himself that, come next Lent, he would quit again. Forever.

He waited until he thought everyone had arrived, then joined them. Midway through his greeting, he stopped. She was back--Jane Doe. He couldn't keep from staring. There was something about her. Catching himself, he began the class, speaking more from notes than with his usual spontaneity. Every time he looked up, his attention locked on Jane Doe. She was always staring at him, understandable, but her expression was quizzical, searching

He hurried through an abbreviated talk. "Before we adjourn, are there any questions?"

Nick was at the ready. "I saw you in the courtroom today when two guys from this parish were arraigned for murder. If you want to help them, you should--"

"That situation is not an appropriate topic for us, and you know it."

"I don't know it. It seems to me that if someone is in trouble, their church ought to try to help."

"Let me decide this church's responsibilities."

The church's responsibility. His responsibility. How much responsibility did he have for the scene in court today?

Philip cringed, visualizing Leonard's jubilant face. Nick had finally managed to unsettle him. Trying to hide his discomfort, Philip moved on. "Look over the sheets I handed out. We'll talk about them next week."

"I didn't mean to start an argument, but as a member of this parish--"

"Mr. Crane, I didn't know you were a member." Philip regretted the sarcasm before the words were out of his mouth.

"Father, pardon me. I thought the church was open to everyone."

Philip could feel his face getting warm. He wouldn't respond until he was in control, but he didn't need to respond. Jane Doe responded for him, telling Nick to stop being a nuisance. "That's what you are. A nuisance," she repeated. "Can't you see you're upsetting him?"

"I have a legitimate concern. If someone has information that might help those two, people ought to listen."

"Class dismissed," Philip said briskly. "I hope to see all of you next week."

"So much for trying to help," Nick said. He stomped out, and the others followed--all except Jane Doe.

She remained seated. Her mouth twitched, as if she wanted to say something and couldn't get it out. Without speaking, Philip sat down on the chair next to her. He crossed his arms over his chest, stretched his legs out in front of him, and stared straight ahead.

Minutes passed, then he said, "Will you let me try to help you?"

When she didn't answer, he continued: "We could start with your telling me your name."

"My name, my name," she repeated. "I don't know my name. I don't know who I am. Did you hear that? I don't know who I am, but I think..." She caught her breath. "I think I'm your daughter."

CHAPTER 13

"It's a girl!"

Philip phoned from the lobby of the hospital. When his father answered, he shouted the news. "Dad, she weighs seven pounds. She has lots of dark hair, and she's adorable."

He started a dash back to the maternity wing, then detoured into the gift shop. He was selecting a small bouquet of spring flowers when he noticed a doll. It was about eight inches high and had a yellow dress and big yellow bonnet. "I'll take that little doll," he said.

When he peeked into her room, Susanna was sitting up, In her arms was their child. It was the most exquisite picture he had ever seen.

Setting his gifts down, he accepted the little bundle Susanna held up to him. He had never held a tiny baby before and should have been nervous. Instead, he felt a confidence, a certainty, unlike anything he had ever known. He had helped bring this human being into the world. It was his right, his responsibility, to protect and raise her.

"Phil, I hope you like her, because they won't let us leave her. We have to take her home." Her usually lively voice was weary, yet even now she made him smile.

"If we have to take her home, we have to decide what to call her."

Sighing, his wife leaned back against a pillow. "Dominique," she said, her eyes fluttering shut. "Dominique Rockcastle, a perfect name for an angel."

The memory of what he did then would remain forever vivid. Without thinking--without planning--he poured water from a bedside pitcher into a cup. Holding his precious bundle in one arm, he wet the fingers of his other hand and sprinkled a few drops of water on to her forehead.

"In the name of the Father, Son, and Holy Spirit, I baptize you Dominique."

In an emergency, anyone could perform a baptism, but this was not an emergency. Philip couldn't understand his action-- not until later. The baby started to cry, and he kissed the damp forehead. "Dominique, you're God's baby now."

A nurse appeared and hustled his daughter out of his arms. "You can come back later, Dad."

Dad. He had never expected to be called Dad. For years, his goal had been to be called Father. Romance and marriage were not for him.

His friendship with Susanna had been casual. When he told her he was studying for the priesthood and said goodbye, he expected never to see her again. He returned to the seminary, never doubting he would forget her. To his surprise, she kept finagling her way into his thoughts. At odd moments, he would find himself remembering their conversations. If anything amusing happened, he could hear her laugh.

When he talked to his confessor about her, he accepted that he was being tested and asked God for help. Again and again, he told himself he had simply enjoyed a friendship. He repeated it like a litany: *It hadn't meant anything. He had never kissed her. It had not been a romance. He was not in love.*

At Thanksgiving, he was granted special dispensation for a visit home because his mother was ill. Susanna had probably forgotten their brief friendship, but he needed to see her one last time. He had to prove to himself that it was true: She hadn't meant anything to him. He hadn't meant anything to her.

Driving his brother's car, he twice almost turned back but somehow kept going until he was at her house. Going up the steps to the veranda, he paused and looked around at a neighborhood of old, but well-kept houses that would have been grand in their day. He felt strangely out of place and wondered what he was doing there. Wavering, he took a deep breath and touched the bell. He waited. Maybe, she wasn't home. Maybe, coming here was a mistake."

"Phil!"

Standing in the doorway, they stared at each other. Instead of inviting him in, she stepped outside.

He had intended a casual, *I'm home for the holiday and thought I'd stop and say hello.* Instead, he blurted, "Do you miss me?"

Her voice trembled. "I'm trying hard to forget you."

"I'm trying to forget you, but I think about you all the time." Philip was confused. This was not what he had planned to say. He had persuaded himself she would hardly remember him. Instead, she was crying. He was saying he'd had to see her again.

A sharp wind sent snow flakes swirling. She hadn't put on a coat. When she shivered, he took her in his arms to warm her. She looked up at him. He bent his face to hers. The touch of their lips was fleeting.

Tears rolled down her cheeks. "Phil, why did I have to meet you? Why did you go away?"

He kissed her again and, in that gentle kiss, doubt vanished. "Susanna, I will never go away again."

They stood close a long time, very aware but not talking until she tugged his hand. "Come inside."

A year later, instead of his receiving the Sacrament of Ordination, he and Susanna received the Sacrament of Matrimony. Charles was his best man and told him, "I always thought if a girl lured you away from the collar, she would be a demure, saintly type. I'm glad I was wrong. Susanna makes her presence known. She's good for you."

His brother was right. Susanna taught him more about himself than soul searching ever could. He had lived in a shell; a veneer had separated him from the world. Susanna smashed through and rescued him. He was a better person because of her, a better person than if he had become a priest. Now, they had a precious little daughter to share and love.

They took their baby home to a tiny apartment on the campus of the small town college where Philip taught Latin and history. She was an unbelievable joy, but her predawn wails kept them awake. Susanna adored motherhood but soon looked exhausted.

They planned a trip home and looked forward to showing off their daughter, surely the most adorable baby ever born. When Susanna's mother wanted her to come home a week earlier than scheduled, Philip reluctantly consented. Her mother would make sure Susanna rested, and he would remain on campus preparing for the summer session. He dreaded the loneliness, but it would only be for a week, only a week.

His daughter wasn't a month old when he took his family to the bus. The trip would be little more than a hundred miles, and Susanna's parents would be waiting.

Inside the depot, Susanna struck up a conversation with another woman cuddling a baby. She would have someone to talk to on the journey.

As the bus started to load, there was a cloudburst and crack of thunder. Rain poured down in sheets. Using his jacket as an umbrella, Philip helped Susanna board. When she was seated, he kissed his daughter's forehead and then Susanna.

"Phil, I love you."

Those were the last words he heard her say.

CHAPTER 14

"You had a daughter. You have to remember her."

Philip jerked to his feet. "I had a daughter. I don't know how you found out about her, but she is dead. She died--"

"On June 30th, eighteen years ago," Jane Doe blurted. "A bus went off the road in a thunder storm. Wasn't that what happened? I checked newspaper archives. I found an article that said a baby identified as Jill Kolchek was found alive in the wreckage. That's me. I'm Jill Kolchek. Only...I don't think I am."

Philip yanked her up, squeezing her arm tight. "What are you talking about?"

"The paramedics, the people at the hospital, they were wrong. They made a mistake. I think I'm the baby they thought was killed. I think my name is Dominique Rockcastle."

Suddenly, her expression changed. "Dominique Rockcastle," she whispered. "I never said it before. It sounds so strange, and it should have been my name."

The first time he saw her, something tugged at him. He realized she was troubled and felt a personal need to help her. Now, all he felt was suspicion. She was treading on precious and painful memories. Releasing her arm, he said. "I don't know how you found out about my daughter, Miss Doe but—"

"That's not my name."

"Why did you say it was?" he snapped.

"When that white-haired guy handed me the sign-up sheet, I started to write Jill Kolchek, the same as always. Then I was afraid. I had to think of another name, and Jane Doe..." Her voice trailed.

"You had nothing to be afraid of."

"I thought you'd be suspicious if you remembered the name from when you read about the accident."

The accident. Two words jolted him back to an abyss where faces loomed, lips made sounds like rustling dead leaves, and breathing seemed hardly worth the effort. He shook his head. "The name would have meant nothing."

"I couldn't be sure, and I didn't want you to wonder about me. I was never going to come back. You're a Catholic priest. That's weird. But I had to see you again. There's something I have to know."

Grasping her chin in his hand, he tilted her face up. He hadn't let himself acknowledge it before. Now he did. She resembled

Susanna. No, it was more than a resemblance. He had realized it the first moment he saw her standing at the door. She looked like Susanna.

Opening his eyes wide, he continued to stare. He told himself he had to be imagining it. Only he wasn't. The resemblance was real. Breathing hard, he released her chin and dropped back in a chair. "My God," he murmured.

"There is something you have to tell me."

He felt disconnected, in a dream state. Could she be right? Could she be Susanna's child? After all these years, was it possible?

"Her birthday," she demanded. "I need to know her birthday."

"Her birthday?" Confused, he murmured, "Whose birthday?"

"Dominique's birthday. Please, I have to know."

It was an effort to think, but she was demanding a birthday. He tried to focus. "May, she was born in May, on the twenty-eighth."

"May 28! I thought I was Taurus, but I'm not Taurus. I'm Gemini, the sign of the twins. That fits, doesn't it? The sign of the twins--two people? Jill Kolchek and Dominique Rockcastle. I said the name again, *Dominique Rockcastle*." Her voice trembled. She had always seemed tense and was losing control.

Philip dealt with emotional people all the time. Advising them to stay calm rarely worked. Patience and understanding were more effective, but he had to calm himself before he could soothe her. Folding his hands in his lap, he closed his eyes. His prayer was wordless. He needed stillness.

Opening his eyes, he was calmer and told himself her resemblance to Susanna could be in his mind. What she was claiming could not be true, but she had to believe it. Why else would she think his daughter's birthday determined her sign of the Zodiac? She had mentioned another date, June 30, the day that determined his life.

Dazed, he found himself reaching for a cigarette, but the pack was in the kitchen. He couldn't leave her alone while he went to get it. She now knew the date she had come for and might bolt. Even if he managed to find her later, he couldn't wait. He had to know now. "Come with me," he said.

In the kitchen, he took fresh cigarettes out of the refrigerator and was lighting one when she held out her hand. The words, "You shouldn't," died unspoken. Silent, he gave her a cigarette and held the match for her. It registered inanely that if the incredible were true, if this girl were actually his daughter, the first thing he had done for her was light a cigarette.

Pointing her to a chair, he sat down facing her. Despite all logic and sanity, hope was stirring. He fought giving in to it. He had seen his child in a casket. The memory was like a tableau forever frozen in time.

Tears had blinded him as strong arms led him down an endless aisle toward a white casket that was too far away yet much too close. Blinking hard, he had forced himself to look. Susanna's face floated behind a mist. Their baby, dressed in the bonnet and christening dress she had never worn, was cuddled in her embrace. He could still hear the echo of his own anguished cry.

Only Charles' tight grip had kept him from taking Susanna and the baby in his arms.

If it had been the wrong baby, wouldn't he have known? It had been up to him. None of the relatives who joined him at the casket and mingled their tears with his had ever seen his daughter.

Philip reached to flick ash on a saucer. The extended hand trembled and seemed remote, hardly his own. He watched the girl take a deep drag and slowly exhale the smoke. The match he held had not lit her first cigarette.

"I want you to tell me everything that makes you think you're..." He could not say he words.

She started to cry. He refused to react. His own emotions needed all his control. When she stopped crying, he asked, "How did you get the idea that you were...who you said?"

"It was right after Mom's funeral. That's why I started to cry. All of a sudden, it just all came back."

"When was her funeral?"

"Last spring, two days after my birthday. Her voice caught. "Two days after the day I always thought was my birthday."

"I'm sorry about your mother. Why did her death make you think you were someone else's daughter?" He couldn't lose control and kept his voice brisk.

"When Mom died, my Aunt Merle said there was something she had to tell me, something she could never let anyone know when Mom was alive. She wanted to tell me right away. She said if she waited, she would never have the courage."

What did she tell you? Philip thought the words, too transfixed to say them.

"Aunt Merle was listening to the news and heard about a terrible bus accident. She was sure it was the bus my mother planned to take."

She paused, and Philip choked out a command for her to continue.

"She checked with the police. They didn't have Mom's name listed and said she had either been killed or taken to a hospital. She rushed to the hospital, praying that's where she'd find her.

"She did find her." Philip said, more statement than question.

She nodded. "Mom was badly injured. She would never walk again, but she was alive. A doctor said she had to have emergency surgery and might not make it. She was crying and begging to know about her baby."

Tears loomed again, and she fumbled through her purse. Philip thought she was looking for a tissue, but she took out a cigarette. "I have only two left," she said.

"When they wheeled Mom into surgery, my aunt walked along side the gurney holding her hand. She told Mom her baby was fine. She hadn't seen the baby. She didn't know how it was, but she had to comfort her sister." Her voice rose. "She had to! That's why it happened."

Philip's chest was tightening. "Why *what* happened?"

"They said Mom's baby was being checked out in the emergency room, and they let her see me. I looked different. She told them I wasn't the Kolchek baby. Do you hear that? I am not who I thought I was."

She talked faster and faster. "When Aunt Merle said there had to be another baby, a nurse held her arm and took her to the morgue. A towel covered a baby girl lying on a metal table. The nurse lifted the towel. The baby was wearing a dress and bonnet Aunt Merle had made. It was her own work. She couldn't be mistaken. The dead baby was her niece."

Philip closed his eyes, remembering. There was another woman with a baby on that bus. She and Susanna had taken seats close together. Shaking his head, he grabbed the girl's hand. "If the babies had been misidentified, the mistake would have been corrected as soon as your aunt told them."

"You don't understand. Aunt Merle was afraid that if Mom knew her baby was dead, she wouldn't fight to live. A nurse said they hadn't been able to save the dead baby's mother. One mother and one baby were dead. One mother and one baby were alive. My aunt never told anyone what she knew, not until she told me."

A band was tightening around Philip's chest. "When your mother saw you," he said, his voice choking, "she would have known you weren't her child."

She shook her head. "Mom was in the hospital a long time. She was in a cast and couldn't move much. They let my aunt hold me up for her to see. By the time she was getting well, I guess I was the baby she remembered."

"Your father--he would have known."

She drew herself up. "He never paid any attention to me when I was little. Later, well," she said, her voice bitter, "he paid me more attention than I wanted."

"Have you told him you think a mistake was made and—"

She interrupted. "I haven't seen him in a long time. I never talk to him. It's like I never had a father."

Suddenly very calm, Philip laid his hand over hers. "You have a father now."

CHAPTER 15

She was alive. His daughter, Susanna's daughter, was alive. It was a miracle, a blessing, beyond anything he had ever imagined. Doubt about her story was gone. Philip believed, but it was a strange belief, like in flying dreams when he knew he could soar over trees.

The phone was ringing. Philip couldn't release his daughter's hand to answer. After five rings, the machine picked up: "Father, this is Mary Kennard. Ernie had another heart attack. The doctors say it's bad. We're at Saint Elizabeth Hospital." Her voice choked. "Father, please come."

The hospital always had a chaplain on call, and St. Aloysius Church was right down the street. Another priest could be there in minutes, but the Kennards were his parishioners. He was the priest they wanted. He was needed and would not let them down.

He started to tell his living, breathing daughter that he had to leave but didn't know what to call her. He would never feel easy calling her Jill. That name was a horrible mistake. Dominique? Maybe, on a glorious day in the future, it would feel right to call her Dominique. Not yet.

A memory surfaced. He and Susanna had been staring in awe at their brand new daughter, naked and unwrapped for her bath. Susanna had commented on how pink she looked. "Our little rosie," she said. They had both laughed and began referring to her as Little Rosie.

He let go of her hand. "A parishioner needs me, Rosie."

"Rosie?" She looked blank.

He grinned. "I'll explain someday. For now, Rosie is what I'll call you."

He dreaded parting with her, but the Kennards were waiting. "Where are you parked?" he asked. "I'll walk you to your car,"

"I don't have a car. I'll take a local bus to the subway. I should hurry. At night, it can be a long time between buses. I've been stuck waiting all alone."

"You won't wait alone tonight," he said. "After I'm finished at the hospital, I'll drive you home."

She shook her head. "It's a long way. You'd have the long drive back and..."

He interrupted. "I'm driving you home." He was her father. She was not one of the many good people who called him father. He and Suzanne had loved each other, and their love had created her. It was late in the day to begin, but he wanted, he needed, to look after her.

He picked up the black, leather case with the items he needed for administering the sacraments, then took her to his car. On the drive to the hospital, they were silent. A million questions, a million things he wanted to say, ran through his mind, but awareness that his daughter was sitting beside him made speaking almost irrelevant.

Approaching the hospital, he did focus enough to ask where she lived.

"I'm staying on the Southside with a friend of my aunt's," she said. "I stay with my aunt sometimes, but since Mom died, nothing is permanent."

Pulling into the parking lot, he said, "You can't smoke in the hospital. I'll show you the area in back where it's allowed." He handed her his cigarettes. "If you must," he added, trying not to sound authoritative so soon.

He was with the Kennards for almost an hour, first administering the sacraments to Ernie, afterward sitting with his wife. "Mary, Ernie has pulled through before. Let us pray and ask that he comes through this. We know it is in God's hands. We accept His will."

Accept His will. How many times had he tried to believe those words after the accident? It was God's will that his wife and baby daughter had been taken. It had to be, but suddenly something was wrong. Only his wife had been killed. A misidentification at a hospital had deprived him of his daughter. God hadn't taken her. She was alive.

"Father?" Mary Kennard looked puzzled.

"What is it, Mary?"

"You look so--well, happy. You keep smiling."

He had just administered the sacraments to her critically ill husband. It was inappropriate, but he laughed. "Mary, Ernie is going to get better. God won't let us down today."

When Mary Kennard went back to sit with her husband, Philip headed to the parking lot. On the way, he passed an elderly nurse he had seen on other occasions. She said, "Hello, Father."

Susanna's daughter was waiting for him. Exuberant with the joy of it, he grabbed the nurse in a bear hug and swung her around. Her glasses slipped down her nose.

"Father!"

He laughed, probably even more surprised than she was. Explanation was impossible. Apology wouldn't cut it. He said, "It's a great day to hug someone," and headed out the door.

"Here," his daughter said, returning his cigarettes. "I only smoked one."

She was only eighteen, too young to be heavy into cigarettes, not that there was an appropriate age. He would have to talk to her, but it was too soon to offer guidance. He certainly couldn't hold himself up as an example.

He had planned to drive her to where she was staying, but at Outer Drive, he turned north, not south. She didn't seem to notice and commented on the scenery.

"The skyline is breathtaking," she said, "I didn't know it was such a beautiful city."

"The place where I'm taking you is on the lake. There will be no bus rides tonight."

She didn't question him, and their banal conversation about the scenery helped Philip hold on to reality. This wasn't a dream. It was happening. He prayed, *Please, God, let it be true. Let her really be our daughter.*

Turning off the drive, he followed a tree-lined road that wound past large homes on sprawling lawns illumined by ornamental lamps. He slowed at a house where glowing torch lights bordered a long, circular driveway. "My brother and his family live here. They'll put you up tonight." It wasn't a question. She didn't have a choice. He needed to know exactly where she was. "You can phone and tell your aunt's friend you're safe and won't be home tonight."

"Her place is a boarding house. No one will notice if I'm not there. But I can't stay here. I don't have anything with me, not even a toothbrush."

"They'll take care of you." He parked in an area in back reserved for overflow from the garage, then led her to the front door.

He hadn't given any thought to how he would introduce her. He couldn't say, by the way, Charles, the baby we buried with Susanna was actually Jill Kolchek. This is Dominique Rockcastle, your niece. "You can be Rosie to me," he said, "but for now, I think I'd better introduce you as Jill Kolchek."

She laughed, the first time he heard her laugh. "Rosie, Jane Doe, I don't care. Jill Kolchek is the name I've answered to all my life.

Approaching the front door, she gasped. "This is a mansion. Does your brother rob banks?"

"He doesn't rob banks, but I think some people believe his line of work is akin to robbery." He added a cheerful, "Don't quote me," and pressed the doorbell.

The housekeeper opened the door. "Father Rockcastle!"

He greeted her, and she said, "I'll let your brother know you're here."

The family's keeshond padded over, too well-trained to sniff but was inching closer when Charles called out, "Philip, I'm in the rec room."

Philip led the way to a recreation room with a pool table, a chess set with four-inch tall pawns and eight-inch kings, a large-screen television, and Philip's favorite toy, an old, one-armed bandit rescued from Las Vegas. The room was not his brother's usually hangout. He was more apt to be in the den in an over-stuffed chair that could have been rescued from the Salvation Army.

Philip was on the most incredible high of his life but needed to sound casual. He couldn't tell his brother about his miracle until he was more in control. Hugging the nurse had made him realize how on the edge he was.

"What are you up to in here, Charles? Shooting a little pool?"

"Yes, trying to keep pace with your niece." He extended his hand to Philip, but his gaze was riveted on the girl.

"Charles, this is Jill Kolchek, a member of my catechism class. I told her she could spend the night here if that's okay with you."

"Your catechism class," Charles said, quizzical. He seemed to catch himself. "Miss Kolchek, a pleasure. I'll get my daughter down here to meet you." He was offering them something to eat when Charlene burst in.

"Uncle Philip!"

"Charlene, please take Miss Kolchek upstairs and show her around."

"I want to talk to Uncle Philip and--"

"Charlene, you can talk to him later."

His daughter caught the command in his voice. After a quick introduction, she hurried her new acquaintance--her cousin, Philip told himself--out of the room.

"Okay, what's up? You're about to jump out of your skin."

Philip dropped a coin into the one-armed bandit and pulled the handle. Watching the reels spin, he said, "She was going to miss her bus."

A cherry and two oranges.

"So you brought her out here? That doesn't make sense."

Philip knew it was too soon to tell Charles she was his daughter. His heart believed, but he needed proof. His brother wouldn't believe. Without proof, no one would believe.

"Phil, if Jill Kolchek is going to spend the night, I think you should tell me why she's here."

He was bursting, Despite his resolve, he couldn't hold it in. "She goes by the name Jill Kolchek, but she's actually...," He took a deep breath. "She's Dominique Rockcastle."

Before his brother could respond, he said, "Charles, there was another woman with a baby on that bus. After the accident, the babies got mixed up. The only person who knew was an aunt. She didn't tell, not until now."

Even to his own ears, Philip sounded frantic, but he couldn't stop. The whole story spilled out--how something about her caught his attention when she came to his class, how the aunt had recognized clothes she made. He told all of it.

After a long silence, Charles said a soft, "I see."

"I brought her here, because--well, I couldn't just drive her someplace and leave her. I need to know where she is."

"I'll make sure she is taken care of," Charles said, his voice still soft. He took two brandy glasses from the liquor cabinet.

Philip shook his head. "Nothing for me."

Charles set the glasses down. "Philip, I know you believe what you're saying. It's wonderful," he paused. "Wonderful, that is, if it's true. I think you should be cautious. I don't want to see you hurt again."

He handed Philip a cue stick. "Let's have a game and talk."

Philip took the stick, aware that Charles wanted a distraction to hide his skepticism.

"How long have you known her?" Charles broke, banked a shot, and a ball made a steady roll to the pocket.

"She came to my class last week. I didn't know who she was until tonight."

"How did she find you?" Walking around the table, Charles chalked his stick. He might sound casual, but Philip realized his brother was mentally in court and preparing his cross-examination. The questions were piercing:

How did she find him? How did she find out about his class? Did Philip know if she had ever been in legal trouble?

Philip didn't know all the answers and could only repeat what he had already said. If Charles was not convinced the girl known as Jill Kolchek was really his daughter, it didn't matter. Someday, he would believe. Someday, everyone would believe.

He put his cue stick down. "I'll go upstairs and say goodbye"

"Wait! We have to talk and--"

Philip kept going. "I'll talk to you tomorrow."

The two girls met him at the top of the curved staircase. Charlene was quick with a hug and instructions to come back soon.

His daughter stood behind her cousin. When he opened his arms to her, she hesitated. "Rosie," he said. She moved toward him. He caught her in an embrace. Gently, he kissed her forehead just as he had the last time he saw cradled in her mother's arms.

CHAPTER 16

Jerry Finlay had enough experience to know his hunches usually led in the right direction. The hunch bugging him now said Haldero and Wilson were innocent. According to his brother, the priest thought so too, but the Roman collar wasn't influencing him. He doubted a likely, street-smart guy like Haldero would partner with a fog head like Wilson. It could happen, but Haldero's reaction hadn't come off like a courtroom performance.

He was sprawled in his apartment's only upholstered chair. Pippa was biting at his shoestrings. If he didn't feed her soon, she would position her teeth on his ankle to show she meant business. He shooed her away. She would have to wait.

All he had to do to fulfill his assignment was let Rockcastle know what evidence the district attorney had. It didn't seem like much, except for Wilson's confession. After he collected his fee, he could forget about the case but, despite himself, he was intrigued. After thinking about it, he decided there was nothing to lose by going on the hunt.

After he fed Pippa, he dug a scrap of paper with a phone number on it out of his wallet. He dialed, and Joyce Cole answered on the first ring. She sounded more gushy than surprised. After a minute or two of banter, he asked if she was familiar with the John Hancock."

"Isn't he the guy who signed his name so big on the Constitution?"

Jerry chuckled, then realized she wasn't kidding. "I thought he autographed the Declaration of Independence, but who cares. The John Hancock I'm talking about is a building. The restaurant on the ninety-second floor serves some of the best food in the city." He started to say that the view from the windows extended half-way to Canada, but checked himself. She might not be a good candidate for hyperbole. Instead of mentioning the view, he used a word he thought would grab her. "Classy, it's very classy."

"What should I wear?" she asked by way of acceptance.

Jerry didn't see himself as a fashion consultant. The best he could do was assure her whatever she chose would look attractive. He jotted down her address and said he would try for an eight o'clock reservation.

His choice of restaurant had been more calculated than just wanting another order of the lobster thermador he had relished there on his first and only visit. An impressive, unhurried atmosphere would keep her relaxed and talking. She would gladly volunteer everything she thought was relevant. If he were going to catch hold of anything, he suspected it would be a detail, a bit of information she might not credit with being important.

He managed a last-minute reservation and, getting dressed, wished he'd had his only good suit pressed. The pants looked a bit rumpled but would have to do. Instead of driving, he hailed a taxi. He wasn't paying the meter. This outing would enhance Rockcastle's expenses. Why put up with the parking hassle?

Joyce's address was an apartment building, and she was waiting outside. The earrings she wore had an even longer dangle, and her fur coat was slung over her shoulder Hollywood style. Getting into the taxi, she edged close to him. He realized her expectations for the evening might be different from his, but hers might not be so bad.

At the John Hancock, they identified themselves to the doorman, then waited in the lobby until a guide wearing a tuxedo ushered them into the elevator reserved for restaurant guests. They rode up alone. Each party was exclusive, and they were greeted by the maitre'd.

"Good evening," he said, greeting them with deference. "Antonio will show you to your table."

"This is my kind of place," Joyce whispered.

He started to ask if she and Bart enjoyed the city's better restaurants, then decided she wouldn't look so dumbstruck if accustomed to fine dining.

Their table was next to a window where the magnificent view of city lights was bordered by vast expanse of lake. Joyce glanced out the window, but her attention seemed more focused on the restaurant or, more accurately, their fellow diners. Her stare was not too discreet. She would never make good at undercover work.

"Jerry, look at the woman over there. The necklace she has on—"

Jerry cut her off. "Look out the window. Better yet, look at the menu."

The menus the waiter was placing before them were in over-sized, handsome folders. While Joyce stared at the impressive folders, Jerry ordered a bottle of Chardonnay, intending the mild, white wine to be their only alcohol. A glass or two might help her reminisce, but too much might uncork emotion. He didn't want a crying jag over her bereavement or, more likely, a temper tantrum because the good life she expected wasn't going to happen.

When the wine was served, she was impressed with the cut-crystal glass and ran her finger along the design. He suggested she order the lobster thermador, assuring her it was always excellent. He needn't tell her he had only sampled it once.

The lobster lived up to his hype, and conversation lagged while they ate. The dish was new to her, and she paused between bites to say how delicious it was. He had to agree with her. It was even better than he remembered.

He didn't lead her to his topic of interest until after coffee was served. "I've been wondering about the annuity Bart expected. I don't know if I can do anything, but that's no reason not to try."

"You should be able to do something. You're a cop."

"Retired."

"You said you do detective work."

"Right. If you want me to help you, you have to tell me everything you know about Bart. The good stuff and the bad stuff."

"How did you know there was bad stuff?"

"I didn't, but most people have a loose bone or two in the closet, even if the bones don't make a skeleton. So tell me, what was Bart's bone?"

"It was before I knew him. He worked in an office, real estate I think, and didn't turn over money when he was supposed to. The way he told it, he thought he could replace it soon, but soon didn't come soon enough."

"Did he do time?"

"I think a few months and probation. Nothing too heavy, but he said would-be employers paid more attention to his record than his diploma from Yale."

Jerry looked up. "Bart Corbin graduated from Yale?"

She nodded. "It's a college somewhere in the east. Maybe New York."

"Maybe Connecticut," he said. Nothing about her suggested she would connect with the Ivy League. It was a lead to pursue, and he asked about Bart's Yale contacts. She was vague. He didn't have any, at least none she knew about.

"Joyce, tell me everything Bart said about the annuity," Jerry asked, more convinced than ever that the so-called annuity was a planned shake-down.

She repeated what she had already told him. "I got carried away when I told you all the things we were going to do. He did mention a cruise, though."

A waiter was leading a couple past their table. Joyce suddenly leaned over, seeming to peer at the floor.

"Joyce, did you drop something?"

Sitting up, she shook her head. "I just had to get a better look at her shoes. They're beautiful. I couldn't afford to buy one shoe like that."

"Joyce, what in hell would you do with one shoe?"

He signaled the waiter and asked for the brandy list. Rockcastle would pay a big tab, and the only information it bought him was that Barton Corbin graduated from Yale.

CHAPTER 17

Philip had traveled the same route many times, but suddenly nothing was familiar. The lights along Outer Drive had a strange radiance. The traffic and scenery seemed like illusions. He was in a surreal world. The only reality was his daughter. Susanna's daughter was alive.

When he pulled into his driveway, the surreal feeling was still with him. Time seemed distorted. It was hard to remember that this morning he had attended court to hear an arraignment. All memory of the day was obscure until he heard the words, "I'm your daughter."

He sat in the car a long time. When he finally went inside, number three glowed red on the answering machine. So what? Messages could wait. They belonged to another reality.

Upstairs, he took a carved wooden chest out of the bottom drawer of his dresser. It held his most valued treasures and was never out of his keeping. The contents both comforted him and broke his heart.

Setting it gently on the nightstand, he lifted out pictures one by one. Their wedding pictures--Susanna had truly been as adorable as she remained in memory, but had he really looked that young? The picture of them cutting their wedding cake always jabbed. They were so jubilant. He smiled at pictures from their honeymoon, a three day excursion to the Lake Michigan Dunes.

Holding each to the light, he studied the photos of their baby. The first one was taken when she was only hours old. He had looked at it so many times, he could envision the little face perfectly with his eyes closed. This time he hunted for a likeness to the girl who claimed her identity. He took an especially long look at a picture of their baby nestled in his arms. Was there a resemblance to Jill Kolchek? He couldn't be sure, but it didn't matter. Their precious baby was alive. It was true. He desperately wanted it to be true.

He wanted to see every picture ever taken of her. There would be pictures from her first birthday. It would have been Jill's birthday, not Dominique's, but they were within days of the same age. Her school photos, he wanted to see them all. What schools did she attend? What were her favorite subjects? His excitement growing, he wanted--he needed--to know everything about her. He had to fill in the blanks of the lost years.

Hurrying to his desk, he started a list under the heading, *Dominique*. He wrote rapidly: photographs, schools attended, favorite subjects, favorite foods.

He jotted down questions: Did she enjoy watching fish? Susanna thought they were fascinating. Perhaps, she would let him take her to the aquarium where he had taken her mother. Susanna's favorite color was green. Was it her favorite color?

He would show their daughter pictures of Susanna and tell her about her mother. How would he describe her? Loving, kind, playful? Descriptions could never convey what she had been. All he would say is that her mother and father had loved each other very much.

When he finished composing his list and wandering through the past, dawn was at the ready. He needed to get some sleep before early Mass, but there was one more thing to do. He took out his cigarettes, broke each one in half, and threw them in the trash. He would never light another. He had to be an example for their daughter.

Not until he got in bed did he realize how totally exhausted he was. His eyes closed. He was sinking into welcome oblivion. Tomorrow would be a good day, a great day. Then it hit him. He bolted upright and stared wide- eyed into the darkness. If he had known his daughter was alive, he would never have become a priest.

CHAPTER 18

Jerry Finlay reached his arm out from under the covers and picked up the phone. He wasn't happy to hear Joyce Cole wish him an eager good morning. They had shared a good dinner and enjoyed a little tactile recreation, but she was part of an assignment--a former assignment if he wanted to be accurate. He didn't want a place on her "call anytime" list.

"Joyce," he mumbled, "it's early."

"You said to let you know if I found anything."

"Yeah." It was the best he could do.

"I was going through Bart's things. D'you know, in the closet I found a suit I never saw him wear? It's dark blue and nicer than the one I took to the funeral home. Of course, he was cremated, so what he was wearing didn't matter."

It was like listening to Sandra. She was the prettiest of his ex-wives, but it could take her upwards of five minutes to tell you a phone call had been a wrong number. He sank into his pillow.

"When he moved in, I didn't let him bring his battered arm-chair," Joyce continued, "but I found room for his dresser. I searched it this morning, and that man had enough socks to last ten years. And shorts! I can't imagine why he had so many."

She had phoned at dawn to give him an underwear inventory. He thought she was finished until he heard a breathy, "That's when I found it."

He roused himself to do his part. "What did you find?"

"My hand brushed against a metal box taped to the top of a drawer. I needed a knife to pry it loose, and I broke a nail getting it open. I won't have time to redo my manicure before I go to work."

He cut her off. "What was in the box?"

"A ring. It looks like a class ring, and it might be from Yale."

"You told me Corbin graduated from Yale."

"It's a man's ring, and it's engraved MOM. Those weren't Bart's initials, so maybe they're just supposed to spell "Mom," like for his mother.

"Why do you think it might be a Yale ring?"

"On the front there's a gold Y over a U. To the side, Yale is embossed in tiny black letters."

"A shrewd bit of detective work," he said. "Was there any-thing else?"

"I'm getting to it." She paused again. He prepared for a dramatic delivery.

"There's a big envelope. It's taped shut and doesn't weigh enough to have anything in it except paper. It could be money," she said, her voice getting eager. "I'm going to open it."

She might toss aside something significant, and he snapped, "Don't open it! Let me have a go at it first."

She agreed to meet him on her way home from work. He would buy her dinner. This time a hamburger establishment would provide the ambiance. He named the place and was seated in a booth when she arrived. As he rose to greet her, she planted a kiss on his cheek.

"Here it is," she said, handing him a nine-by-twelve Manila envelope. She slid into the booth. "Do you think it might be important?"

"Corbin must have thought it was."

"I spent all day hoping there was something in there about the annuity."

Jerry knew her intelligence wasn't sterling but was still surprised she could think an annuity was a finders keepers deal. "Here," he said, handing back the envelope. "You do the honors."

She tore it open, then pulled out a small envelope and a folded piece of newspaper. She turned the Manila envelope upside down and shook it once, then gave it another shake. Nothing fell out. She slumped back in the booth. "It's just a letter," she complained.

"Let me read it." He took the envelope and, inside, he found a folded sheet of blue-lined paper torn from a notebook:

Hey Bro, Thanks for remembering I spent Thursday night in your dorm. I owe you big time for that and for getting my jacket. Can't figure what happened to my ring. Stupid to take it off, but there's nothing about it in the news. I don't know when, but I promise to square with you.

It was unsigned and had a brief post script: *Destroy this note.*

Unfolding the newspaper clipping, Jerry read an advertisement from a plant nursery: *Spring flowers, Tops in Quality, Lowest in Prices.* No one could think that was worth saving, but the article on the reverse side bought Jerry Finlay's attention.

He read it twice. A woman identified as Patricia Lazarus had been found stabbed to death. Personal effects found with the body led police to the restaurant where the victim was employed. A co-worker reported that Lazarus had talked as if she expected to be married soon, but did not know the name of the man Lazarus was dating.

For Jerry, a scenario was falling into place: *What if MOM had been involved in the Lazarus murder? He removes the ring, possibly to wash blood off his hands. In a panic, he forgets the ring and his jacket. He sends Bro to get them. If Bro is Corbin, he delivers the jacket, but keeps the ring and the note.*

"Are you listening to me?"

"Joyce, I'm listening, and I want you to tell me everything."

"The waitress needs our order."

He looked up. "Just a hamburger, fries, and a cup of coffee."

"Don't you want a beer? I'm going to have one."

"Sure, a beer," he said.

"Something in that letter sure got you going," she said, more accurate than usual.

"I'm working for a lawyer whose brother thinks the men indicted for Bart's murder are innocent."

"But you can still help me find out about the annuity."

He shook his head. "If the annuity Bart talked about was actually his plan for a shakedown, there is no annuity."

"What's a shakedown?"

"It means that you have someone over a barrel. They do what you want or else you rat them out."

"It's like blackmail."

"Just like blackmail."

"I don't understand. So what if someone wanted Bart dead? How would that prove those guys didn't murder him."

He grinned, for once impressed with her thinking. Taking a fresh look at her, he decided that if she took off some of her make-up, she'd be nice to look at. No! He banished the thought. She might be attractive, but he didn't have time or inclination to walk that road again.

"Joyce, if I turn up evidence that Corbin was trying his hand at blackmail and those two go to trial, the defense can suggest someone else had a reason to kill him. More important, it will give me something tangible to take to Charles Rockcastle."

"Who's he?"

"The lawyer I do work for. I'm sure the priest at the arraign-ment is his brother."

The waitress stood ready to put their orders on the table. Jerry folded the letter and newspaper clipping and slid them back in the envelope. He wasn't a do-gooder, but if that priest was right, two left-over citizens that society ignored were going down for something they didn't do. He hated to admit it, but the case was intriguing.

CHAPTER 19

Philip stared at a reflection. It was his own face, but he felt detached. He hadn't awakened *from* a dream. He had awakened into a dream.

Yesterday morning, he hadn't known he had a living child. She was a joy beyond anything ever imagined, but there was something else, a vague feeling, not quite defined, that told him life could never be what it had been. He finished shaving and dressed, but the routine activities didn't dispel the sense that this was a different reality. It lingered with him when he entered the church.

Don Cianca was serving the day's Mass and waited in the vestry. Without giving his usual morning greeting, Don announced, "Father, I have something important to tell you. I talked to Nick

Crane. He's not a parishioner, but I think you know him. He has thick blond hair and--"

Philip cut him off. "I know Nick Crane. Any conversation with him can be put on hold for now."

Actually, any conversation with Nick Crane could be put on hold forever. Philip tried, but couldn't like the man. On occasion, he had added Nick's name to his prayer list, as much to assuage his uncharitable feeling as to bless the man.

He donned his investments and followed Cianca into the church. As he intoned the opening prayers, he thought he could feel Susanna's presence. She was rejoicing in heaven, knowing he had been reunited with their daughter.

On weekdays, he made announcements but didn't give a sermon, a homily as the Church preferred it be called. After reading through several routine announcements, he concluded with the usual reminder about his Wednesday night class.

He fell silent, Several minutes passed. What was he waiting for? He didn't know and was surprised when the words came pouring out: "I want everyone to join me in a prayer of thanksgiving for something wonderful that has come into my life. I have a daughter. For years, I thought she had died in a terrible accident when God called her mother home. Yesterday, I found out she had been spared. She didn't know her true identity until recently."

He hadn't intended to share his miracle but, once he started, he couldn't stop. Talking at a gallop, he told it all, from the death of a wife he loved--surely a surprise to his parishioners to learn he had once been married--to his grief at her death, to his return to the seminary, to a reunion with a daughter he had thought was dead.

When he finished, there was silence, then a sound. At first Philip didn't recognize it, then he realized someone had the audacity to be clapping in church. The sound increased amid a shuffling of feet. People were standing up and clapping. Even old Mrs. Komac in her usual, front pew seat, struggled to her feet. Someone called out, "Praise God!"

Never before had Philip witnessed such a spontaneous and joyful reaction in church. It was unprecedented. The question that had plagued him through the night was answered. These were his people. They cared about him. His joy was their joy. No matter how he had been led to this altar, it was his place in the world.

"Father," Don Cianca, seated in the high-backed chair to one side of the altar, caught Philip's attention. "It's time," he whispered.

Philip understood. Attendees at weekday Masses often had jobs or other commitments. He had to keep to the schedule. "Thank you for sharing my blessing," he said. "I will never forget your love, but our deacon thinks it is time to continue." He turned back to the altar.

"Ite Missa est."

When the Mass was over, an eager group gathered at the door.

"Father, I'm so happy for you."

"Thank you." Philip knew her but was too keyed up to grab the name. It didn't matter. Someone was interrupting.

"Father, did you become a priest because your wife was killed?"

"God's will," he murmured. "God's will."

It was Mrs. Komac's turn. She face was tear-streaked, her touch on his hand gentle. "Oh, Father, will your daughter attend Mass here? Will we get to meet her?"

"I hope so." He stopped. Had he caught a glimpse of someone standing just beyond the church steps? There was no time for a second look. A volunteer who helped out at the church elbowed close, launching more questions.

"Father, I don't get it. Why didn't your daughter know who she was? How did it happen?"

"God's will," Philip repeated.

Finally making his way to the vestry, he found Don still waiting. "Don, you still here? Won't you be late for work?"

"There's something I have to tell you."

Philip laughed. "You want to tell me something about Nick Crane. Okay, let's hear it." In his new world, Nick Crane might be a great guy.

"Nick's not why I waited. I just have to tell you..." His face tensed; his eyes squinted shut. Philip expected a repeat of expressions of shared joy. Instead, Don's words sounded like a pained confession.

"Father, you don't know, I never told you, how much I wanted to be a priest. It was all I thought about. When the seminary accepted me, I was overjoyed."

His frown deepened. "I don't know why, but I lost my calling. When the final step was right in front of me, I left."

"Don, you lead a good, Christian life and shouldn't regret--"

Don interrupted with a determined, "I don't regret anything! I love Judy. I love our kids. His voice slowed. "But it's not the same. That's why what you told us today got to me. God had to mean for your wife to die and for you to be separated from your daughter."

Don grasped Philip's arm. "God wanted you for his priesthood. He needed you more than He needed me. I'm happy for you. Judy will be happy." His grip tightened. "You're so lucky, so blessed. I know it's wrong, but I guess I'm envious."

Philip jerked away. *Lucky, that he had endured a tortured grief for Susanna? Blessed, that he had lost years of knowing and loving their daughter?*

His exuberance faded. He didn't feel lucky. He didn't feel blessed. That vague feeling had a name. He felt betrayed.

CHAPTER 20

The exuberance was gone. Philip walked back to the rectory, seeing only the scatter of autumn leaves cluttering the ground. He didn't look up until he heard her voice.

"Father."

He had not been mistaken. Tara had been at the church. This was the first time he had seen her since Octoberfest when he resolved to put her out of mind. He started to say Tara, but caught himself.

"Mrs. DeVeccio."

She smiled, and he tried not to remember how he thought her smile enhanced a pretty face.

"Father, your daughter--it's wonderful, amazing. I'm so glad I was here."

"I thought I saw you."

"I came because I need to talk to you." Her voice trailed. "I don't think it's right to trouble you now."

Her hair, instead of hanging loose and framing her face, was pulled tight and fastened in back. Though she had never seemed to wear much make-up, today she looked too pale to be wearing any. Even smiling, she looked tense. Something was wrong, and she had come to him. Despite himself, he was glad.

He opened the door to the rectory. "My daughter doesn't change my concern for my parishioners. How can I help you?" He was pleased to have kept his manner routine.

Leading her to his office, he said, "If you can suffer my coffee, I'll get you a cup. Do you take cream or sugar?" The question was a deliberate effort to sever the past. He knew she drank coffee black.

She declined the coffee and sat down, taking the chair his daughter had sat in when she identified herself. He couldn't resist telling her.

"Yesterday evening, the girl sitting in that chair told me she was my daughter."

"In this chair?" She smiled. "I'm so happy for you, happy for her, too, but it had to have been an incredible shock."

"I haven't gotten over the shock."

"Do you think you ever will?"

It was a serious question. He tried to answer. "I don't know. Right now, I doubt it. Tara, everything has changed. I can't explain it, but I feel it. It's more than just knowing my daughter is alive. It's a different world." He shook his head. "I'm not making sense."

"It makes perfect sense, at least it does to me." She hesitated. "You told me you had been in love. I didn't know you'd been married. Her death--what a terrible thing for you."

Despite his intentions, he could feel himself slipping into the comfortable feeling he always had with her. It would seem natural to tell her about the private ache and loneliness that never left him, words only his confessor had ever heard.

He caught himself. "Mrs. DeVeccio, if you tell me the problem, perhaps I can help." It was a much used sentence and reestablished their formal relationship.

She looked away. Whatever she had to tell him wasn't going to be easy. "I don't know if I can tell you."

"I'm sure I've heard worse."

"This involves you, and it's not your fault."

"Involves me?"

"Of course not. At least, not really. It's my former mother-in-law. She went to Children's Protective Services and reported me as an unfit mother. She's trying to get custody of Derek and David. In my heart, I know she can't do it, but she's causing as much trouble as she can."

Philip started to tell her she had nothing to worry about. Anyone who had ever seen her with her sons knew she was a thoughtful and loving mother. He could attest to that. He had seen her and her sons many times.

Many times.

The thought registered. "Does this have anything to do with my visiting you?"

She gave a barely perceptible nod. "I guess the old witch keeps tabs on everything I do, hoping to come up with something."

"And she came up with me."

"I hate to involve you, but I got a call from CPS. The complaint filed against me says I have men visiting me at all hours. Philip, that's absolutely not true."

He didn't want her to call him Philip. It was sliding backward to a time he had left behind. She must have sensed it, because she continued, "Father, in the complaint it says I entertain men. They can be seen smoking on my porch. You're the only one."

"I know that," he said, not needing her to reassure him. "I can't believe an unsubstantiated report is anything to worry about. No court would considerate it sufficient grounds to interfere with your custody."

"A social worker phoned. She wants to set up an appointment to talk to the boys. I'm afraid that if she does--"

"They'll mention me," he said.

"There was nothing wrong with your visits. The boys didn't know, they couldn't know, how I felt." She glanced away. "To them, you were just a friend. I'll instruct them never to mention you."

To them you were just a friend. Her words underscored what he already knew.

"Don't tell them to lie," he said, trying not to appreciate her implication. It was a tense moment. He was relieved when the phone rang.

"Father Rockcastle," he said, answering.

"Father, Bishop Corday would like to see you at four this afternoon. Can I tell him you'll be here?"

Philip knew phrasing it like a request was a courtesy. A summons from the bishop was to be obeyed, but such short notice was surprising. "Yes, of course," he said, drawing a star on his day planner. He usually would not have needed to write down a same-day appointment with the bishop, but the last twenty-four hours had left him strangely detached. The world he knew was off in the distance. He would need a reminder.

His attention was caught by a carefully printed word in the list of activities for the previous day: *Court.*

It hardly seemed possible that a scant twenty-four hours ago he had attended an arraignment. He had thought it important to be there. Now, it was hard to remember.

Although recollection of the courtroom might be dim, suddenly one thing was clear. There was nothing he could do to help Haldero. He had made a promise he couldn't keep. His face must have reflected the realization.

"What's wrong?"

"Tara, nothing's wrong," he said. "I was just thinking about something that happened yesterday."

"The court hearing for the Wilson kid."

Again, she displayed her uncanny ability to know what he was thinking. "So much already coming at you, and then I show up to involve you in something else." She looked weary, but her unexpected smile was genuine. "Think about your daughter. She's all that matters."

They looked at each other. Philip felt himself revisiting the warm place he had shared with her in the past. He wanted the feeling to linger a few moments longer, but the phone rang again. Reluctant, he picked it up. "Father Rockcastle."

"It's me."

"Rosie," he said, still unsure of what to call her. "Where are you?"

"I'm still at your brother's house. I hope it's okay to phone."

He laughed. "Dear, you can call me anytime"

Tara tapped the desk for attention. When he looked at her, she was smiling. Her eyes glistened with tears. She left the room, letting him talk to his daughter in private.

Philip didn't care how long he stayed on the phone. He didn't care if the world stopped turning. He was talking to his daughter.

CHAPTER 21

Charles couldn't leave for the office until he had a chance to talk to the girl alone. If a client had to wait, he could count on Persy to offer coffee, croissants, and a convincing excuse until he arrived.

Deciding he needed the caffeine, he poured a second cup of coffee. He never lay awake at night reviewing a case, especially if the next day would see him in court representing a client in a major action. The tougher the case, the more he needed the confidence of a good night's sleep.

He wasn't confident now. It had been a long, troubled night. Philip wasn't a client. He was the little brother Charles always looked after. He was intelligent enough to have excelled in law school, but he was too trusting, never more so than now.

Analyzing the situation, Charles decided the girl couldn't be Philip's daughter. Perhaps, she had learned about the accident from old newspaper articles, either saved by someone she knew or from the archives. More difficult to fathom was why she would claim a dead baby's identity.

Was she after money? Not likely as the daughter of a Catholic priest. Was it media attention? Possible, but with attention, she was likely to be found out. Nothing he came up with made sense, but one thing was certain. The longer Philip believed her, the greater the pain when he learned the truth.

Someone was coming downstairs. He was confident it wasn't Charlene who excelled at being a late sleeper. It had to be the girl. He could almost hear a black-robed figure say, "Your witness."

She looked tense and stopped at the foot of the stairs, still clinging to the banister. Charles went to her, placed a hand on her shoulder and kissed her cheek.

"Good morning, my dear," he said, taking her arm and leading her to the breakfast alcove. "Did your cousin provide you with everything you needed?"

"My cousin? Oh, you mean Charlene."

He nodded, noting that a relationship to Philip's niece had not occurred to her.

"She keeps extra toothbrushes. She gave me one, and this is hers." The girl indicated the blouse she was wearing. "It's so new she had to cut the tags off. She wants me to keep it, but I don't think I should."

"Of course, you should keep it. Green suits you," he said, pulling out a chair for her. "Let's you and I have breakfast and a nice chat."

She pulled back. "I'm not hungry, but I hoped..."

"Hoped what, my dear?"

"Could you spare a cigarette?"

"I smoked my last one," he said, snapping his fingers in regret. He didn't mention that his last cigarette had been ground out for decades. "What's your brand?"

She shrugged. "Viceroys, Marlboros, whatever." "I'll phone the market and have them send some over."

The girl stayed in the alcove while he phoned the market. "I want a carton of Marlboros," he said, talking loud for her benefit.

Marge was at her mother's for a few days, but Charlene might try the novelty of getting up early. He hurried, knowing he might not have much time to make his case.

A DNA test would be definitive and, with her in the house, a sample of her DNA would be easy to get. As Philip's sibling, he could use his own for a comparison. Unfortunately, getting the results of a test might take a week or more. Every day that he believed she was his daughter would add to Philip's pain when he learned the truth.

A plate of doughnuts and bread rolls were on the table. When she said yes to a cup of coffee, he poured one from the urn on the sideboard and placed it and the cream and sugar tray in front of her. He took a seat where he could get a clear view of her face. Taking depositions and in the courtroom, he had learned that flash reactions could be far more revealing than long responses.

"You and Charlene are close to the same age," he said, never losing his smile. "She graduated from high school last June. I suppose that's when you were donning a cap and gown,"

"Cap and gown?" It took a moment, then she said, "Of course, I would have graduated from high school in June, too. I mean, well, I did."

"Charlene graduated from the St. Mary Academy. It's all girls. I think she would have liked boys in the curriculum. Was your school co-ed?"

She nodded vigorously. "Oh yes, we had guys."

"What school was it?"

"Just a small school," she said quickly. "I'm sure you never heard of it."

"Where is it?"

"In Ashton, where I grew up."

"Ashton," he mused. "Where's that?"

"About a hundred miles south of Chicago."

"Were you born in Ashton?"

Before answering, she took a sip of coffee, clearly framing her answer. "My father was stationed in Germany. That's where I always thought I was born, but I guess I was born in the States."

When a client was lying, it was usually best to behave as if all was believed. Defenses came down; responses were more spontaneous. That was when he had a shot at finding out where reality was located. It was obvious she was not a recent high school graduate. She had probably shaved a few years off her age to match little Dominique's year of birth.

He studied her features. If you expected to find it, you might detect a resemblance to Susanna, but not the strong resemblance Philip claimed. Charles knew the human mind had the ability to see what it expects to see. His brother wanted to see Susanna. He didn't.

The girl broke a doughnut and dipped a piece in her coffee. "I like this room. The white table with red chairs and the walls in red and white makes me think of peppermint candy," she said

"I'll have to tell--" he hesitated--"your aunt Marge you like it. She did the decorating."

"She's good at it. I bet that's why you didn't hire a decorator, not because they're expensive," she said, an unexpected eagerness in her voice.

"Yes," he said, answering the question she hadn't asked. "we could afford a decorator."

"I'm sure of it," she said. "I've never been in such an elegant place before."

While she attended to her doughnut, Charles considered how to proceed. She was apparently price-tagging her surroundings, but he was still certain she couldn't think being the suddenly undead daughter of a parish priest could provide a financial windfall. She had something else in mind. The sooner he knew what it was, the better. Priest or not, his little brother still needed his protection.

He leaned back in his chair. "It's wonderful that you discovered your true identity. Tell me how it happened."

Seeming reluctant to answer, she took another bite of doughnut and looked away. Charles waited, then she said, "After my mother died, my Aunt Merle told me I was misidentified at the hospital. At first, what she said didn't seem real, but I couldn't stop thinking about it. I wanted to find out who I was--or at least, who I should have been."

"Did you aunt tell you Philip's name?" He could refer to his daughter as her cousin, his wife as her aunt, but couldn't bring himself to refer to his brother as her father.

"I read newspaper articles about the accident that my aunt had saved."

As he had suspected, her information came from the newspaper. At least, she was truthful about that.

"That's where I found his name--and her name." She closed her eyes. "Dominique Rockcastle," she murmured.

Opening her eyes, she continued. "I looked Philip Rockcastle up on-line and was shocked to find out he was a Catholic priest."

She was repeating what Philip had told him, but he needed to hear her rendering to see if one day later her story had changed. "After your Aunt Merle--sorry, what did you say her last name was?"

"Shultz. There's no C in it. It annoys her when people spell it with a C."

"After she told you what had happened and you located Philip on-line, did you phone him and tell him who you were?"

"I didn't want to talk to him. I just wanted to see what he looked like."

"So you went to his catechism class. How did you find out about it?"

She sipped her coffee, "A couple of Sundays ago, I went to his church. He was at the altar, and the woman next to me told me who he was."

"You had seen him. If that's all you wanted, why did you go to his catechism class?"

"He said anyone could attend." She hesitated. "I'm not sure what I was thinking, but he looked so peculiar in church clothes. Vestments, I think they're called. I wanted to see him when he was dressed like a real person."

She smiled. "During the class, he seemed like a nice guy. That's why I went back again, yesterday."

Her expression changed. She was either putting it on, or her thoughts had turned sad. Her smile gone, she said, listening to him, I wondered what it would have been like if he had been dad to me instead of Father to everyone."

She sounded sincere, but Charles had heard too many well-rehearsed lines to be fooled. Her story about graduating from high school recently was a lie, and she was almost surely lying about her age. Dominique would be Charlene's age, This girl definitely looked older. If she were lying about her age, none of her story could be true.

The doorbell rang. Charles answered and took the cigarettes from the errand boy. Returning to the breakfast alcove, he noticed how sunlight beaming through the window caught the girl's hair. In the play of light, the dark brown shade took on an auburn cast. Memories stirred of someone else whose hair looked auburn in sunlight. Who was it?

He shook his head, refusing to give way to imagination. It would be wonderful, beyond belief, if Philip and Susanna's daughter were alive, but that was the problem. It was beyond belief.

"My dear," he said, handing her the carton of cigarettes. "Let me get my camera. I want to take pictures of you."

Charlene was bounding downstairs. She could be in the pictures too, but his daughter's face wasn't the one he needed.

CHAPTER 22

Philip didn't have time to think about his summons to the bishop's office until on the way. It wasn't a long drive, but slow traffic gave him a chance to wonder. If anything as major as a transfer were imminent, it would be a scheduled conference, not an almost "come as you are" command. Pulling up at a red light, he banished the thought of a possible transfer. He loved his parish and was secure in the thought that he was in the right place, serving his church exactly the way God wanted.

The priest at the desk in the reception room was an old acquaintance recently elevated to monsignor. Greeting him, Philip bowed his head a moment in honor of his new rank. "Hello, Ed, I have an appointment."

"Father Rockcastle." Interrupting, the new monsignor sounded unexpectedly formal. "His Excellency is waiting for you."

Philip opened a heavy, oak door and entered a large office where an enormous desk was centered on a round, red carpet and surrounded by several upholstered chairs. An impressively framed painting of the pope was prominently displayed. Bookcases with glass doors lined the walls.

Bishop Corday was seated on a tall-backed, black chair. Hardly looking up, he indicated the large armchair facing him. Although not as tall as Philip, he had an imposing presence. His hands always caught Philip's attention, the long, slender fingers moving gracefully in frequent gestures.

The atmosphere in the room was uneasy. Suddenly apprehensive, Philip sat down. The silence seemed long before the bishop leaned back in his chair, laced his fingers together, and stared at him.

"Father, when we first heard the story, we doubted it. Unfortunately, now we've heard it repeated and must take a position."

Philip was at a loss. "Your Excellency, what story?"

"Do you mean it's not true?"

"I'm sorry. I don't know what you're talking about."

"We have been advised," the bishop said, stressing each word, "that, from your pulpit, you announced you had a daughter you knew nothing about."

Stunned, Philip slumped backward. "Do you mean you summoned me, because I told my parishioners my daughter was alive? That's not possible. Your office called hardly an hour after I shared the news."

"I believe someone at your Mass texted the story to a TV station. A pushy reporter contacted us for validation."

The bishop continued, and Philip caught a hint of sarcasm. "Perhaps, Father, you are unaware we live in a high-tech world."

"I never thought that--"

The bishop didn't wait for him to finish. "Of course, you didn't think. You made an announcement without informing us first. We were caught off guard. I believe we managed to quash the story. I don't think that excuses you for going public with something potentially damaging to the church."

Philip sat up straight. "I didn't think of it as going public, and it certainly can't damage the church. It was spontaneous. I hadn't planned to, but I shared a miracle with my parishioners. Bishop, they were thrilled, delighted, for me."

"Indeed. I understand they broke into applause." This time, sarcasm was unmistakable.

"Father Rockcastle, you have to realize how hatefully the story can be construed. A Catholic priest announces from his pulpit that he has a grown daughter he didn't know about? It will be too easy for people to think you had a little love child stashed somewhere. Our enemies and gossip mongers will pounce and create yet another scandal."

Philip stiffened. "I should have notified you first. That's reasonable. But there is nothing scandalous about my having a daughter. Certainly, I knew about her. Her mother and I had a valid, Christian marriage."

He fought a surge of anger. "I thought our child died in the accident that killed my wife. He paused, trying for the name to use--"*Dominique* didn't know her true identity until--"

A wave of the bishop's hand silenced him. "Yes, indeed, that's the story one of the callers told. I know your background, of course, and know it's true. However, with our enemies rejoicing at the negative situations that frequently plague the church in these Godless times, we have to be careful not to create another potential scandal. Gossip doesn't seek out the truth. Our critics will try to make something of it."

"Let them," Philip said.

"What?" It was more gasp than question. The bishop gestured with both hands, his right index finger coming to rest pointing at Philip. "It is our responsibility to guard and promote the reputation of the church. I shouldn't have to tell you."

"Bishop Corday, you don't have to tell me. I would never willingly do anything to damage the church," Philip said, still fighting anger. "My daughter is a blessing, a miracle. I want the church to rejoice with me, not think I've been irresponsible."

Spreading his fingers wide, the bishop placed his hands on the desk and leaned forward. "If you are contacted by the media, refer them to us. It is my apostolic instruction that you tell no one else about this."

This--the knowledge the child he had grieved for was restored to him was rendered simply as *this*.

Philip took time framing his response. "Bishop, I will not talk to the media. However, I must inform my family and my wife's family. They have a right to know."

"You betray the church if you continue to report a situation likely to create disparaging rumors and--"

Philip had heard enough. "Do I have your permission to tell family?"

His tone indicated he would, with or without permission. The bishop waved his hand, this time a gesture indicating both consent and dismissal. "Enough," he said.

Philip stood up but didn't move toward the door. Waiting, he studied the confident, regal figure behind the desk. The bishop opened a folder and picked up a gold pen.

"Bishop Corday," Philip said, his voice soft, "would you like to give my daughter a blessing and send her a message?"

The bishop looked startled, then smiled. "Yes, please do. Tell ah--" he paused, "Dominique, I will include her in my prayers." He added, "Father, despite this misunder-standing, I want you to know the church rejoices with you."

The words soothed, and Philip left through the heavy oak door.

CHAPTER 23

Jerry put Pippa's breakfast of Friskies into her bowl while listening to phone messages. He wasn't paying close attention and had to play Chuck Rockcastle's message a second time:

"Finlay, forget about Wilson and Haldero. I doubt we can help them, and something more important has come up. I need a complete report on a woman named Jill Kolchek. She says she's from Ashton."

On first hearing, Finlay hadn't caught the name of the town. Now, he jotted it down: *Ashton.*

"She claims to have been born in Germany, which may make her birth records difficult to check. But if she attended high school in Ashton, they should have her place of birth in their records. Also, I need to know when she was enrolled. She claims to be eighteen, but I think she's at least twenty. She says her mother died last spring. Presumably, the woman's last name was Kolchek, and there's an aunt named Merle Shultz. I'll upload a photo to you. My daughter is on the right. I need to know everything you can find out about the girl on the left."

Suddenly, Rockcastle's voice changed. Even on a recording, he sounded worried. "Time is critical. Reach me by cell phone, not the office number." There was a pause then, "Thank you."

Rockcastle paid well, but Jerry usually didn't get a thank you from him. It underscored a sense of urgency. He didn't hesitate accepting the assignment, and Rockcastle surely knew he would. A response could wait until he had something to report.

He started on it right away, doing an internet search for Merle Shultz and Jill Kolchek that yielded nothing, not even a phone number. He would have to check out the town. According to MapQuest, it was a hundred and twenty miles south of the city. Autumn was in full swing. It might be a pleasant drive, but it was Friday. School records wouldn't be accessible over the weekend. Meantime, Jerry wasn't ready to call it a day on the Bart Corbin murder.

It would take a big rock sailing through the district attorney's window to get him to reconsider his case against Wilson and Haldero, but Jerry's cop instinct nagged that the right rock was out there. The priest thought they were innocent, and the mainstay of the prosecution's case was the Wilson confession. Jerry's reaction to the Wilson kid was that he was just as likely to confess to stealing the Statue of Liberty.

Coffee was the fuel Jerry needed for heavy duty thinking, and his own brew wasn't going to cut it. He bent to give Pippa a farewell stroke but she sauntered away. A typical female, affection on her terms only.

It was a short walk to the cafe, reached through a hallway in a commercial building and hardly visible from the street. Most of the customers were regulars. As he reached his table, Tessa was already there with his coffee. "Haven't seen you for a few days," she said. "Been busy romancing the ladies?"

"Not for a long time, Tessa."

She laughed. "I don't believe you. I know what cops are like."

"Tessa, I'm an ex-cop."

"That doesn't mean you're an ex-lover.

"This ex-cop has a lot on his mind, and it isn't women."

He downed the coffee while she got his breakfast--the usual, scrambled eggs, hash browns, and double toast. He was dipping the last of his toast into his second cup of coffee when Tessa wedged into the chair across from him.

"You look like more of a grump than usual," she said.

"You think I look like a grump? Now, I can't tell you I think you're losing weight."

She laughed. "You wouldn't have anyway, but I shouldn't have called you a grump. You look distressed or something. Running this place, I hear lots of problems."

"And now you want to hear mine? Tessa, you're as good as a bartender."

Her cheeks widened in a smile. "Try me."

"You nosy broad, the divorce lawyer I do investigations for pulled the plug on a job that has me intrigued. I expected to see it through."

"Through to what?"

He shrugged. "I don't know."

"It doesn't sound like a divorce."

"It's not."

"So what kind of case is it?"

Jerry didn't have a confidant. Joyce would listen, but anything going in her ears might get lost in an abyss. It wouldn't hurt to use Tessa as a sounding board.

"Tessa, it's a murder. Two young guys are going down for it, and I have a nasty hunch they're not guilty. The lawyer doubts it, too. That's why he gave me the job, but now he has a higher priority."

"Is the new case a divorce?"

Jerry shook his head. "Doesn't sound like it, but I don't know."

"Is the murder something I would have heard about?"

"The case didn't get as much coverage as an expected rain storm. A bum was found dead in a park. Only..."

"Only what?"

"I don't think Bart Corbin was a bum. He had a decent place to live. He owned several suits and a big wardrobe, yet the police report describes him as wearing old pants and a ragged shirt."

That puzzled him the most. Joyce had described Corbin as clothes conscious and always particular about what he wore. Why would a man who wouldn't be found dead dressed like a bum be found dead dressed like a bum? What was he doing in Humboldt Park, half-way across the city from where he lived? The drug deal scenario didn't cut it. Every section of the city boasted its own street corner drug kings.

Tessa pulled herself to her feet and went to help a customer at the register. Jerry heard the jingle and was glad when she came back.

"Corbin was there to meet someone," he said, framing the thought. "It was someone he knew. It had to be. The bum persona could have been to keep them from being noticed."

"Why?"

As soon as she asked, he realized the answer. "Because they had a history together. I think something went down a long time ago. Whatever it was, the other guy thought it was time to silence Corbin, and he couldn't risk being recognized. I'll bet you the price of a cup of coffee that whoever killed Corbin had a bum persona, too."

"What do you think it was all about?" Tessa asked, ignoring a call from a man at the counter wanting a refill.

"I don't know," Jerry said, "but it was significant enough for Corbin to decide it was pay up time."

He couldn't be sure, but it made sense if the ring and note Corbin had guarded so carefully belonged to someone he was trying to shake down. "Tessa, Corbin had the goods on someone. Recently, the situation changed and made what he had more valuable." Jerry's own words convinced him and would explain why Corbin told Joyce his annuity was finally going to pay off.

"Do you think that's why he got murdered."

"That makes sense to me."

"Where do you go from here?"

He shrugged. "Nowhere. The district attorney regards the case as solved. The lawyer who hired me closed his checkbook."

"Can't you go at it on your own?"

"Not a good idea. It would be on my time and with my money."

"Finley, you're aching to do it."

He took another slug of coffee. "Chances are, I wouldn't come up with anything provable."

"At least you'd know."

"What would I know?"

"You would know you tried. Finlay, you're a cop. I bet you sleep with your badge pinned to your pajamas."

"I sleep raw and damn it, when I retired, I had to turn in my badge."

To his surprise, talking to Tessa had pointed the way.

He made a decision. Even if Chuck wouldn't be paying him,

He was too caught up to drop the investigation. He followed Tessa to the register, stretched his arms around her big middle, and kissed her.

CHAPTER 24

Nick Crane found himself remembering an old, boyhood ambition he had never shared with anyone. He had wanted to be a detective. Throughout his boyhood, Sherlock Holmes had been his hero and role model, a fact that got him chastised in sixth grade. The assignment had been to write a paper on an important, historical person. He had chosen Sherlock.

His teacher rejected his work, saying Holmes was not a real person. She rebuffed his contention that Sherlock was as real as Thomases Jefferson and Edison, and far more exciting. He had admitted that Edison had come up with some handy inventions, but Jefferson? The Declaration of Independence served a purpose, but he must have spent hours and hours sitting at a desk, writing with a feather.

In imitation of Sherlock, Nick took a magnifying glass with him everywhere. When too young to emulate Sherlock's pipe smoking, he had settled for rolling an occasional Bull Durham. He'd needed a musical instrument and, as one of a large, struggling family, never convinced his mother a violin was a necessity. By making deliveries for the grocer on Saturdays, he had earned money to buy a good harmonica. With surprising ease, he'd learned to play it. Years after the magnifying glass had been set aside, it still traveled with him everywhere.

When old enough, he had enlisted in the Coast Guard. At sea, he had plenty of time to read and, want one or not, he had an audience for his harmonica playing. He liked the coast guard, but mustered out after his second enlistment. By the time he returned to Chicago, he had forgotten about being a detective and found a career in construction. He loved the strenuous activity. He also loved a dark-haired girl and joined the ranks of married men. Marie was a Catholic. That was her business. Through the years, she worried because he was not Catholic. That was her business.

His desire to become a detective was a thwarted but not quite forgotten ambition. He would have been good at it, the best. Attending the arraignment for the Wilson kid and Haldero made him think he might be able to prove it.

He had driven his pick-up truck to the courthouse, paid for parking, and been there early enough to hear everything. Unfortunately, everything hadn't amounted to much, excepting when Wilson entered his guilty plea. Hearing him, Nick's muscles had tightened. This wasn't Sir Arthur Conan Doyle. This was real life, and it might be up to him to prevent an injustice.

Driving home, he had considered going to the police and laying it all out. Would they believe him? Not a chance unless he had something to back it up. Proof had to exist, but he wasn't Sherlock and didn't know how to find it.

Considering all the angles, he had decided his best bet was to explain his suspicions to Rockcastle. If the priest backed him up with the police, his evidence would seem more credible.

He had arrived at the rectory early enough for a private conversation, but that hadn't happened. Not until the class started did he have a chance to mention the arraignment. The priest should have been interested. Instead, he acted as if Nick was trying to be annoying.

Nick was never annoying, never malicious. He did like to study people and ferret out what could be called their unprotected spots and test their reaction to a well-directed challenge. It was legitimate research into human behavior. Rockcastle should have understood that this time he had a different purpose. Instead, the priest blew him off.   Without help from Rockcastle, Nick had to go it alone.

On Friday morning, he put on his suit. Marie asked whose funeral it was.

"I have important business," he told her.

After running his pick-up truck through the car wash, he drove to the William Avenue station. The cops there would be familiar with the case and welcome his input.

In the lobby, a bedraggled woman was seated on a chair by the wall. Getting Nick's attention, she beckoned eagerly. He started toward her and was attacked by a torrent of cuss words.

From behind the glass partition, the desk sergeant called out, "Loretta, any more of that, and it's out you go." He turned to Nick. "Don't mind her. She likes to sit in here when it rains. We let her so long as she behaves."

"It's not raining," Nick told him.

The sergeant shrugged. He had a round, ruddy face and, by Nick's estimate, was about forty, his own age.

"I need to see the captain about a very important matter."

"The captain isn't here. What's it about?"

His information had to be guarded. "Is there someone else in charge I can talk to?"

The officer waved him to the chairs by Loretta but Nick remained standing. He didn't want to sit near her and seem like another person waiting for rain so he could take refuge.

After about fifteen minutes, a sandy-haired officer, name badge Lieutenant Waldon, came to talk to him. Nick needed the privacy of an office, but Waldon stood hands on hips, obviously content in the lobby.

"I have information about the Bart Corbin murder."

Waldon looked him over, no expression, no reaction. His nod was non-committal permission to continue.

Nick cleared his throat. "I think the two guys going down for it might be innocent."

He had grabbed the attention of the desk sergeant and a man and uniformed woman at work behind the partition. At this point, Waldon should have taken him to the privacy of an office. He didn't.

"You think those two are innocent," Waldon said, his voice flat. "How do you come up with that?"

"It's a long story, well, not a long story. But I was near the recreation center the day Corbin's body was found and--"

"What were you doing there?"

Nick hesitated. "Nothing special. Just sitting in back by the boat ramp."

"Just sitting there in the dark?" Waldon asked.

"It wasn't dark. It was afternoon." He had said enough and stopped. So what if he liked to sit under a tree and play his harmonica. There was nothing wrong with that, no one's business but his own.

"What time was it?"

"I'm not sure."

Waldon asked more questions, irrelevant Nick thought. It wasn't the dialogue he had anticipated and wanted to get to the point. He had something important to tell them. They had better listen.

"He was only a few feet away, and called me by my old nickname. That's when I took a good look at him. Otherwise, I wouldn't have recognized him. The shabby way he was dressed, no one would have recognized him."

"What did he call you?"

"Snowball." Instinctively, Nick touched the thick mop that had scarcely darkened since childhood.

Someone snickered. "It fits."

Judging by the look on his face, Waldon wasn't taking him seriously. Annoyed, Nick tried again. "I knew he had to be dressed that way for a reason. I thought there might be a party for bums going on in the boat house."

"A party for bums," Waldon repeated.

"Not a party for bums," Nick said, irritated. This guy wasn't trying to understand. He would have to break it down. "I mean, a party where everyone comes dressed shabby. But that's not what it was."

Waldon wasn't going to take him to an office. Nick had to state his case there in the lobby. He had just started explaining everything again when two officers came in carrying a screaming woman wildly kicking the air.

Loretta jumped to her feet. "That's the way, Honey. Tell 'em. Tell'em.

"Okay, Loretta, that's enough. Out of here." The desk sergeant made a move toward her. Shouting a cheerful goodbye, Loretta scrambled to the door.

As the officers carried their cargo passed Nick, her screams sounded even louder.

The distractions made it hard for Nick to continue, but he tried. "I didn't get suspicious until later when I read about the way Barton Corbin was dressed. I think the two of them had planned a meeting and dressed shabby, because they were afraid of being recognized."

Waldon interrupted. "Why would they be afraid of being recognized?"

Nick started to say they probably wanted to avoid reporters who might be out for a story, but then they would insist on a name. They weren't taking him seriously and would never believe him.

"Hey listen," Waldon said. "I know you want to be helpful, but that case is solved. Those punks were arraigned two days ago."

"That's why I'm here," Nick roared. "I don't think they're guilty. You're not listening. I want to talk to someone higher."

A smart aleck behind the desk called out, "Snowball, maybe, you should take it to the Supreme Court."

That caught Nick up short. His voice dropped to a whisper. "That might be where this is going."

He pushed the door open with a clenched fist. For this he had worn his suit and had his truck washed.

CHAPTER 25

A weather forecaster with a fun house grin was predicting rain for Monday. "Almost an inch is expected in the morning hours. Another storm is expected to come our way in late afternoon."

Jerry Finlay had heard enough and clicked the remote. He had listened to the weather to find out if conditions warranted inviting Joyce on the drive to Ashton. Maybe, she didn't cut it as a witty, engaging conversationalist, but her chatter was usually cheerful and would dilute the boredom of a long slosh through the rain. More important, even if he were off the Corbin case, his curiosity about it hadn't faded. He hadn't given up on the idea that Joyce had information she didn't think was relevant. On a long drive, he might squeeze it out of her.

When he phoned and invited her, she said, "I have to let my boss know I strained my back."

"You strained your back?"

"No, but I haven't taken a sick day in a long time, and I want to go with you."

She agreed to an early start, but Monday morning traffic was already thick when he pulled up in front of her apartment building. She stood under an awning, minus the fur coat and with an umbrella dutifully in hand. The black sky hadn't let go but hovered like a doomsday threat.

He had stopped in the middle of the street. "Quick," he yelled, leaning to push open the passenger door. When she scrambled in, he headed south, glad he was going against the traffic gorging its way into the city.

She turned out to be a good passenger and left off conversation until they were on a fairly open stretch of highway. Then she said, "You mentioned that this trip was connected to a case. Is there a chance you'll find out something about Bart's annuity?"

The rain didn't start with a drizzle but with a sudden cascade that sent blinding rivers down the windshield. Jerry didn't answer until the wipers had cleared a view of the road. "Joyce, I've tried to explain that there never was an annuity. Bart knew something about that murder in the newspaper article and was demanding payment to keep quiet. That's where the money he expected was supposed tp come from."

The only sounds were the pounding of the rain and the squeaky-squish of the wipers. Breaking a long silence, Joyce said, "I wonder if that's what they were talking about."

"What *who* were talking about?"

"Bart and someone he phoned. He was so secretive, going into the hallway and closing the door. I thought he was talking to a woman."

Putting her hand on his leg, she squeezed tight. He didn't mistake it for affection. She was tense and struggling to remember. "I crouched close to the door. I couldn't catch everything. What I heard didn't make sense, but it wasn't like he was romancing."

"Think hard. Tell me everything you remember."

"Bart said he wouldn't be putting himself in jeopardy. That's the word he used. He said it a couple of times. I thought he was laughing. He said he would tell them his conscience had bothered him for years. He said something about the situation changing, and he had to tell the truth. I didn't hear the next part. I think he laughed again and said something like, 'You don't want me to write a book and come off like a hero, do you?'"

"Joyce, this is very important. Did he say who he planned to tell?"

"All I remember is that he said he might have to do his civic duty."

He started to chide her for not telling him this before, but a little late scores higher than never. "You're okay, Joyce. You did great."

Her eavesdropping wasn't hard to interpret. It matched exactly what he had told Tessa. Bart Corbin was threatening someone with exposure, because something happened recently to make his target vulnerable.

"The person he was talking to," Joyce said brokenly. "Do you think he might have, I mean, if Bart wanted money from him, and he didn't want to pay..." Her voice faded.

"Do I think he killed Bart? That makes more sense than thinking the Wilson kid did it. But I told you. I'm not on that case any more."

A northbound diesel truck passed, splashing a torrent of water over the car. It took a moment before the windshield cleared. In that moment, he changed his mind. So what if he was off the case? He was too caught up in it to let go. "Joyce, let's see if I--if we--can come up with something solid to hit the DA with."

He spotted an IHOP near the highway. "I'm hungry. Care for some pancakes? I'll pull up close to the entrance. Get your umbrella ready and make a run for it."

He used a newspaper for an umbrella on his own bolt to the door. When he got inside, Joyce was already ordering his coffee.

"How much farther is the town we're going to?" she asked.

"About twenty more miles."

He took out the photo from Rockcastle. "Joyce, we're trying to check out the girl on the left. She says she's eighteen which would be the age of the baby she claims to have been switched with. Rockcastle thinks she is older. I have the name of the aunt who supposedly made the switch, but I couldn't track her on-line."

A waitress asked for their order. Jerry took a quick glance at the menu. "Pecan pancakes, eggs over easy, and bacon."

"I'll have the same, only..." she paused, "with a waffle, scrambled eggs, and no bacon."

Jerry was amused by her idea of "the same." She faced him now, and he saw a different pair of dangling earrings. If he ever felt the need to buy her a present, he knew what to get.

Joyce studied the picture. "I never worked with a detective before," she said. "How do we do it? I mean, how do we find out if she is who she says she is?"

"I can't check birth records, because she claims the baby she was switched with was born in Germany. All we can do now is find out if the girl in the picture went by the name of Jill Kolchek."

"Wouldn't her social security card and driver's license prove who she was?"

He shook his head. "Not necessarily. She claims not to have a driver's license, and a social security card wouldn't prove her identity. Rockcastle thinks she's lying about where she went to school and figures there has to be a reason."

He finished a second cup of coffee and, back on the road, headed to Ashton. It didn't take long to find the town's only high school. Jerry held the umbrella and cuddled close to Joyce as they waded their way to the entrance.

A girl guard told them they had to get a pass and sent them to the administration office where another girl was staffing the desk.

"I am looking for information about Jill Kolchek. She was a student here and probably graduated within the last couple of years."

Smiling, the girl said, "If she graduated, she won't be here now."

"I understand that," Jerry said, "but I need to know when she graduated and what years she was enrolled."

The smile vanished. She looked blank. "Miss Ellis would know how to find out. She has hall guard duty now."

Jerry was surprised when Joyce asked, "Where are yearbooks kept? If we could find her picture in a yearbook, it would tell us what we need to know."

"Yearbooks," the girl repeated slowly. Perhaps, she had never heard the word before. Suddenly, her light went on. "Yes! You could check yearbooks."

Joyce asked, "Can you tell us where they're kept?"

"There's a set on a shelf in the principal's office. I can't take you there, but I can get them."

She wasn't gone long and returned with a stack of yearbooks. Jerry checked the embossed dates on the covers and opened the most recent. He hunted through it, then handed it to Joyce for a recheck. Fifteen minutes later they closed the last book. There was no Jill Kolchek.

"Are you Miss Ellis?" Joyce asked the woman replacing the girl at the desk. "We are trying to locate our niece. We think she may have gone to school here."

Miss Ellis had pink hair and a long filmy scarf around her neck. Her arm swung in dramatic gesture as she handed Joyce a piece of paper. "Write her name. I will see." She breezed off and returned within minutes. "The computer says no Jill Kolchek attended school here within the last ten years. Do you want me to check further back?"

"Not necessary," Jerry said. Jill Kolchek, if that was her name, had lied about where she went to school.

"What now?" Joyce asked after they returned to the car.

"Only one high school, probably only one post office. They might be able to give us an address for the aunt. If they don't have an address for her, Jill Kolchek's entire story crashes."

At the post office, Jerry Finlay expected another negative--either they couldn't or wouldn't help--and was surprised when the burly clerk on duty had no trouble placing the aunt. He said Merle Shultz lived at 27 Gillette Street.

"What about Jill Kolchek? Do you have an address for that name?"

"That used to be my route, and there was a Kolchek up the street from Shultz, a crippled lady. I think she died."

Jerry waved his thanks, and grasped Joyce's arm going back to the car. Following the clerk's directions, the Shultz address proved easy to find, but no one answered the door bell.

"Let's try a neighbor," Joyce suggested.

Jerry would have checked out neighbors without Joyce's input, but admired her initiative. The rain had let up, and they selected a house across the street. A tall, middle-aged woman answered the door. "Yes, I know Merle Shultz," she told them.

"Perhaps you can help us decide if she is the Merle Shultz a client wants us to find. It's a legal matter. Something about a legacy," Jerry said, choosing an approach he thought would get the woman talking.

She immediately invited them in. "Merle and I are dear friends. She's a lovely person. Be sure to tell her I said so. Tell her I'm happy about her legacy, no matter how much it's for."

She paused, apparently hoping for details. When none were forthcoming, she continued. "Like I said, she's a lovely person, but I have to admit she's a messy housekeeper. That dog of hers is a real nuisance. It runs around while Merle sits on her porch smoking one cigarette after another. I hate to say bad things about her, but she doesn't care if that unkempt front yard of hers brings down the neighborhood."

After the neighbor finished listing her dear friend's flaws, Jerry managed a couple of questions. "Do you know if she has a niece, a woman possibly around twenty years old."

"That would be Jill."

"Check this photo. Does either of the girls look like Jill?"

"Jill is the one on the left. I can't place the other girl."

"That's okay. What's Jill's last name?"

"I don't know, but if it's Shultz she ought to change it. It's an ugly name, and Merle--that's an odd name too, don't you think?"

"Have you ever heard the name Kolchek?"

"Her sister's last name was Kolchek. That might have been Jill's last name," she said, smitten with genius. "She could get around on crutches, but you usually saw Jill pushing her in her wheelchair. Poor Jill, she was always taking care of her mother, and that father of hers! He's a disgrace."

Pulling back a curtain, she looked out the window. "There's Merle now. That dog is with her. She must have been walking it. I wouldn't be surprised it she took it out when it was still raining."

Jerry took Joyce's arm and almost yanked her toward the door. "Thank you, Mrs..."

"Smyth, spelled with a Y. Be sure to tell Merle I helped you. Such a good friend. I hope it's a big legacy."

Merle Shultz greeted them pleasantly. She was short, a little plump, and her smile was inviting. "Of course, Jill Kolchek is my niece, my late sister's daughter." She stopped abruptly. "My God, I hope nothing's wrong. That's why you're here, isn't it? Something happened to her."

Before Jerry could get the words out, Joyce assured her Jill was fine.

"That's right, Mrs. Shultz. Your niece is fine, and she's not in any trouble," Jerry added. "We just have a few questions about her. How old is she?"

Starting to look apprehensive, Merle Shultz said, "She was eighteen in May."

"I'm sure you remember the terrible bus accident," Jerry said. "Your poor sister was hurt so bad, and babies may have been accidentally misidentified. DNA testing is under way and will prove it one way or the other. That will take time, and someone needs to know as soon as possible."

Merle Shultz drew back. "I don't know anything about that. If there was a mistake, if babies were misidentified, blame it on the hospital. It was not my fault. I didn't do it."

"Mrs. Shultz, thank you for your time." Jerry said. He didn't say, "Thank you for telling me what I came to find out." He had been looking for a reaction, not truth, and he got what he wanted. The girl called Jill Kolchek was eighteen, and Merle Shultz had been frightened when he said babies might have been misidentified. He could tell Rockcastle what he wanted to know.

CHAPTER 26

When Philip answered the phone, the response to his "Father Rockcastle," was barely a whisper, but he knew. His grip tightened on the receiver. He should call her Mrs. DeVeccio but "Tara" slipped out. He quickly followed it with a formal, "How can I help you?"

"I'm still worried about my mother-in-law's accusations. I think if you and your daughter had dinner here with me and the boys, it would be obvious we had nothing to hide."

Her reason for the invitation hardly convinced him. The real reason was both troubling and, despite his intentions, pleasing.

She continued, "I would love to meet your daughter. I just know she's a lovely girl."

"She is," Philip said, "and she would like to meet you." Such a mindless thing to say! His daughter didn't know Tara existed.

Before giving himself a chance to decide it was reckless, he said, "I have a better idea. I'm taking her and my niece out for dinner tonight. You, Derek, and David should join us. Dining publicly would certainly..." He didn't know what it would do and couldn't finish.

When they hung up, he phoned and made a reservation for six at the Berghaus. Located in the midst of the downtown area, the restaurant was an old Chicago landmark, one of few that hadn't been swept away by progress and skyrocketing real estate prices. Philip chose it because he remembered the old-world ambiance. It was a special place and this would be a special occasion.

He hoped they could all squeeze into the convertible. It would be tight, but he preferred to take Tara and the boys instead of meeting them at the restaurant.

Bookkeeping, his least favorite responsibility, was delinquent. He recorded bills and expenditures in a hurry to catch up. A visit to a bedridden parishioner was next, then an appointment and a few phone calls. He tried to be as attentive and caring as usual, but his mind was elsewhere.

Charlene had said they would be at the rectory no later than three o'clock. By mid-afternoon, he was ready and waiting. When they still hadn't arrived at five, he had his first experience as a worried father.

It was a relief at five-thirty when the doorbell rang and he heard Charlene's cheerful holler, "Uncle Philip!"

She had parked in the driveway and was ready with smiles and apologies. "I know we're late, but we went shopping. Do you want to see what we bought?"

His daughter followed her inside, carrying packages. "Most of it is for me," she said. "Charlene paid for everything with her dad's credit card. I told her I didn't think she should."

He kissed them both. "I don't think your uncle Charles will mind."

He told them they were going out to dinner. "You'll meet a lady and two boys."

"The boys," Charlene asked, perking up, "how old are they?"

Philip laughed. "Much too young."

He showed the girls one of the bedrooms used whenever he had a resident curate. "You can freshen up in here."

He rarely hid his collar. He was proud of it, but this was a family outing. It seemed reasonable to wear a blue, turtle-necked sweater under a sport coat.

Six people did manage to fit into the convertible, but it was snug. Tara cuddled David next to her under the same seat belt. The girls and Derek sat in back.

"Father, every person is supposed to have his own seat belt. We learned that in health education."

Philip glanced over his shoulder. "What was that, Derek?" Turning back, he caught Tara's eye. They had both heard him, but cozy felt good for one short drive.

The restaurant lived up to Philip's recollection. The tables and chairs were dark, polished wood and deep-red tapestries adorned the walls. A smiling host addressed Philip. "You and your family come this way."

His family. He was dining out with his wife, their pretty daughters and two, lively boys. For this one time, he wasn't father to a parish. He was father to a family and was going to enjoy it.

He started by ordering a bottle of wine. The waiter displayed the bottle with a flourish and poured Philip a taste. At Philip's nod, the waiter filled Tara's glass, then his. Philip raised his glass and gently touched it to hers. The boys had lemonade, the girls colas and, in imitation, there was a cheerful clinking of glasses all around.

"Mom, can I order anything I want?" Derek asked.

"This is my party," Philip said. "You can order anything your mother approves."

His daughter was glancing around looking for something.

"What do you need?" Tara asked.

"I don't see anyone smoking. Do they allow it in a place like this?"

"No, they don't," Philip said, sharper than intended. "It's time for both of us to quit."

His daughter shook her head. "I'm not going to quit. Charlene's dad bought me a whole carton. I haven't even finished the second pack."

Her words were a blow. No way would Charles have loaded her with cigarettes if he believed she was his niece. The gift had to have been a distraction, something to put her off guard so he could find her out. Philip couldn't suppress a frown.

"Philip, what's wrong?"

"Tara, nothing is wrong. I thought of something. That's all."

She touched his sleeve. "You had kicked smoking until the Wilson boy got in trouble. Did talking about cigarettes remind you of him?"

A waiter served the salads. Philip didn't answer and hoped mention of Leonard Wilson was over. It wasn't.

"I heard you went to Wilson's arraignment. Was the lawyer you talked to there? Does he think he can help?"

She had distracted him from the realization that his brother didn't accept the switched baby story, but reference to Wilson didn't help. "Tara." Philip's voice was soft but carried a message: *No more talk about Wilson.*

"I'm sorry," she said. "I wasn't thinking." She added an extra cheerful, "This salad is delicious."

"Girls, tell Tara about your shopping trip. What stores did you make richer?"

The diversion worked. Charlene had no trouble talking about places to shop. His daughter volunteered an occasional, "Everything was so expensive."

"Father." Derek wanted his attention.

Turning toward him, Philip caught his daughter silently mouth the word *father*. It was quick, only a second, but their eyes locked. She didn't feel exclusive. He was father to everyone.

Philip cleared his throat. "Dominique, hand your dad the bread sticks."

It was decided. She was Dominique. He was Dad.

There was no question about whether they would order dessert. The boys had their selections in mind. It was apple strudel for Derek, an ice cream concoction for David. The girls opted for a small dish of ice cream, and Tara said all she wanted was an espresso. "Make that two espressos," Philip told the waiter.

Feeling expansive, he sat back in his chair. The dinner had been excellent, but the warmth he felt stemmed from more than that. He was filling a vacant role. Tara cared for him. The boys needed a father, and his daughter needed a father. No, she needed a dad.

Unexpectedly, Don Cianca's words echoed. "God had to mean for your wife to die and for you to be separated from your daughter. He wanted you for his priesthood. He needed you."

The words hadn't convinced Philip when Don said them. They didn't convince him now. The God he loved and served could not have ordained Susanna's death and his tortured grief. He could not have ordained that Susanna's daughter would grow up without knowing her mother's name.

His thoughts were confusing. It had to be the wine. He shouldn't have drunk the second glass. He would enjoy the rest of the evening, pay the enormous check, and leave a big tip.

Tomorrow, everything would be just as it had been.

CHAPTER 27

Nick was raging mad. He didn't lose his temper often, at least not every day, but those cops were stupid. He wanted to give them information that might nail a murderer and keep a couple of innocent guys from growing long beards behind bars, yet he had been ignored. Worse than ignored, he had been treated like a match for Loretta who came in from the sunshine to stay dry.

He was still seething the next day when he and his crew framed a job. It was usually gratifying to see a structure begin to rise from the ground, but he was preoccupied. He didn't even swear at the truck driver from the lumber yard when he unloaded two-by-fours two yards from the site.

When he mentioned the arraignment, the priest hadn't realized he was trying to help. His best bet now might be to write everything down. If Rockcastle saw it on paper, he would know

Nick was serious. He had a hunch that, working together, they could figure the angles.

When he got home, he told Marie to hold his dinner. "There's something I have to do."

His computer skills were good enough for him to write letters, but it was easier to clarify his thoughts holding a pen. He got out the pad of yellow legal paper he kept for copying poems and items that struck his interest and sat down on a beat-up chair wedged between a heavy dresser and the wall. It was his spot to hunker down when he had a good read.

He wrote the date, then printed the words, TO WHOM IT MAY CONCERN.

Where to begin was a problem. He couldn't just dash off a few sentences telling what he had seen. To give it credibility, he had to start at the beginning.

He had grown up in the area of the city nicknamed Bucktown, said to be short for Bucket of Blood. He wrote the name carefully, decided it was irrelevant, and crossed it out. More important was the time he spent at North Avenue beach, fishing off the pier and swimming. Everyone who hung out there had a nickname. He was Snowball. A scrawny, red-headed kid was Smarty, a choice misnomer. The standout was a tall, dark-haired fellow nicknamed by his uncommon middle initial, Q.

Q once challenged Nick to a race from a raft to the end of the pier. Nick knew he was the better swimmer, but Q beat him. Digging his pen deep, Nick wrote Q's name, a name that lately was showing up in the news. Nick had to get people to listen to him. He owed it to his country.

Chances are he wouldn't have recognized him at the park if Q hadn't been going at a trot, head down, and rammed into him. When Q looked up, they had stared eye-to-eye. Despite the pulled-down hat, Nick got a good look at his face. Even then, he would have had a hard time believing it if Q hadn't cried out, "Snowball?" before he grimaced and took off running.

"Q." Nick had shouted after him, then looked around expecting to see someone in pursuit.

Nick had played it over in his mind a hundred times. What could someone of Q's national importance be doing in Humboldt Park dressed in ragged clothes and an old, slouch hat?

When he first heard about Wilson's confession, Nick had had no reason to question it. The kid was a screwball, and Haldero could have drawn him in. It was only later, after Barton Corbin had been identified, that he started to wonder. Corbin had been educated, a Yale graduate according to news reports, and so was Q. The address given for Corbin was in a high-end area yet, when his body was found, he looked so scruffy, the police suspected he was homeless.

That got Nick thinking. Why would anyone—even a lightweight brain like Wilson--rob and murder someone who looked unlikely to own the price of a hamburger?   Why was Q in the park close to the time Corbin was probably killed? Nick was convinced there was a connection. If he was right, Q could have arranged a meeting with Bart Corbin, and lured him to a place he thought would be safe."

"Nick." Marie had planted herself in the doorway. "What are you up to?"

He waved her off. "I'm busy."

"I can't believe you're writing love notes on yellow paper, but dressing up in your suit and having that truck washed has me wondering." She crossed her arms and stared hard. "Something's up."

It took a minute, then he realized. Marie thought he might be romancing. It was almost gratifying. Hell, it *was* gratifying, but she had nothing to worry about. He admired good-looking women, most men did, but he wasn't on the prowl. He had better tell her the truth.

"Marie, I think I saw someone I used to know right after he committed a murder. What I need to do is — "

Marie cut him off. "Nick, stop reading those sick true crime books. They're making you balmy." Laughing, she headed toward the kitchen.

His wife laughed at him; the police blew him off, and the priest was annoyed. Nick was indignant, but he had something to say and people were going to listen. He finished a page, flipped it over, and continued writing. When he finished, he set the pad aside and went to the kitchen, being careful not to notice that Marie was smirking.

He enjoyed his dinner--pork roast, sauerkraut, and boiled potatoes--a favorite menu. When he finished eating, he went back to his nook, studied his letter, and then crossed out Q's name and his nickname middle initial. He would give up that information later, when his evidence was given credibility. He detached three pages from the pad and folded them so that TO WHOM IT MAY CONCERN showed at the top. It was as good a time as any, and he drove to the rectory.

"Jane Doe," he said, surprised when she answered the doorbell. "This isn't a night for the class."

"The class is on Wednesday." She started to close the door."

"If there's no class tonight, what brings you here?"

"What brings *you* here?"

"I need to see the priest. I have something very important to give him."

"My...dad isn't here," she said.

"Your dad? Jane Doe, does that mean you're the long, lost daughter I heard about?"

"I am."

"Father Rockcastle's daughter...well, I'll be a monkey's uncle."

"There's a strong family resemblance."

After he stopped laughing, Nick said, "You nailed me with that one. Don't be sore at me for teasing you in class. I am tickled for both of you. Marie will be, too."

She nodded. "Everyone is happy for us."

He had intended to hand the letter to the priest, but his daughter would do. "Here," he said, handing her his letter. "Tell him Nick Crane said it was very important."

CHAPTER 28

Charlene wondered why it took her cousin so long to answer the door. "Did you know that guy?"

"His name is Nick Crane. He's just a nuisance who comes to the catechism class."

"A nuisance in a catechism class?" Charlene laughed. "That might pep things up."

Dropping a fold of yellow paper on the kitchen table, Dominique sat down. "At the last class, he upset..." she took a breath, "my dad because he wanted to talk about some guys who had been arraigned. I don't know what that means but--"

Charlene cut in. "It means they were bound over for trial." Her voice faltered. "Or something like that."

"I think my dad was at the arraignment thing. So was the nuisance. He left that," Dominique said, pointing. "I guess it's a letter,"

Charlene picked it up. *"To Whom it May Concern.* I heard Daddy tell Mom that Uncle Philip thinks two guys charged with murder might be innocent. I wonder if that's what this is about."

"When Nick Crane tried to talk about the court stuff, my dad wasn't interested."

"I'm sure he's interested. Daddy said he had his investigator looking into it, because Uncle Philip was so worried. If Nick Crane wanted to talk about it in class, maybe he knows something."

"I wonder what's taking him so long. It was a short drive to Tara's house."

"Cousin, he's in no hurry. He wants to spend time with her. I knew he did. That's why I asked him to drop us off first."

"Charlene, what makes you think he wants to spend time with her?"

"Didn't you see the way they looked at each other when their wine glasses kissed? They're in love." She sighed. "It was so romantic."

"I thought Catholic priests couldn't fall in love."

"They can't get married, but of course they can fall in love. Taking vows can't hold love back. It just makes it beautifully tragic, like Romeo and Juliet or Superman and Lois Lane."

Charlene unfolded the pages. "To whom it may concern," she repeated, "D'you know, Cousin, it may concern us."

"Charlene, don't read it!" Dominique made a grab, but Charlene turned, holding the letter out of reach.

"It's not sealed, and there's no actual name on it," Charlene said, already reading the first page. When she finished, she tried to hand it to Dominique.

"No, I don't want to."

"Go on, Cousin! It's interesting."

Dominique hesitated, then took it. Reading, she shook her head. "I don't get it."

"Nick Crane saw someone in the park," Charlene said patiently. "They called each other by their old nicknames. He was Snowball. The other man's middle initial was his nickname, but it's crossed out. The man was running, like he was trying to escape from something, and it was close to where the corpus delecti, was found. Nick Crane thinks he might be the killer."

"Where does it say corpus delecti?"

Charlene cleared her throat. "It doesn't, but corpus delecti means the body of a crime. Someone was murdered so there was a body. A dead body is a corpse, so it would be a corpus delecti."

Dominique looked properly impressed. "What does Nick Crane want my dad to do?"

"He doesn't say, but he must think Uncle Philip, or someone else who might be concerned, should try to help."

"When he gets back, we'll give it to him and — -"

"I have a better idea," Charlene said, dropping her voice to a whisper. "Let's try to read the name he crossed out."

"Why do you want to do that?"

Charlene was busy. Explanations could come later. She held a page up to the light. "Quick! Write down these letters."

Dominique took something out of her purse. Charlene was surprised to see a cigarette, not a pen.

"You can't smoke here! It's a rectory."

Dominique lit up. "My dad smokes here, so I guess I can, too."

"Not now. Put your cigarette down and get something to write with. We don't have much time."

"I don't think you should do that."

"I'm not doing it. We're doing it."

"I've never had a father before, I mean, not one that cared about me. I don't want him to think I can't be trusted."

"No one will know. So hurry. Get a pencil. We're cousins and we're already best friends. Best friends do things together."

Dominique dug in her purse for a pen. "Do best friends get in trouble together?"

Charlene giggled. "If you trust each other to get into trouble, then you know you're best friends. Uncle Philip knows me. If there's a problem, he won't blame you. Write down M. It's a capital. I think there's another capital M. I'm trying to make out the other letters."

The front door opened. "Charlene, Dominique."

Charlene snatched the scrap of paper Dominique had jotted letters on and shoved it into her pocket. "Uncle Philip," she called, her voice lilting, "we're in the kitchen."

"I'm sorry I took so long." Looking at Dominique, he said, "I thought we talked about not smoking."

"We talked about it," Dominique said, taking a quick last puff and putting her cigarette out.

"Uncle Philip, thanks again for taking us out for dinner," Charlene said. "The shrimp scampi was so good, and I loved the old-fashioned restaurant."

"I'm glad you enjoyed it."

"The little boys were fun, and I liked Tara. I hope I see her again." She gave him a sly look. "She's such a nice person and very pretty for an older woman."

"Tara is only..." He stopped.

"Uncle Philip, don't you think she's pretty?"

"No, I mean, well, I haven't thought about it."

Of course, she was pretty, and he wouldn't hesitate to say it if he wasn't afraid of showing his feelings. Charlene felt triumphant. She had caught him. Raising her eyebrows, she gave him a knowing smile.

Their gaze locked. They understood each other. She had always adored Uncle Philip and now they shared a very adult secret. She had told Dominique he was in love but would never tell anyone else. Well, probably not.

Dominique had refolded the letter. "Nick Crane left this. He said it was important."

"That guy," Uncle Philip said exasperated and picked up the letter.

CHAPTER 29

Q stood on the balcony of his high rise apartment and looked out at the lake. It was an ominous grey, reflecting low dark clouds. The panoramic view took in the harbor where the *Legality* was docked. Gripping the iron railing, he leaned forward. He couldn't quite see his yacht but knew she was out there, a modest token that evidenced he was fulfilling his destiny. His name would be remembered.

Closing his eyes, he turned his face toward the brisk wind. The moist air was cold but refreshing. He tried to think about the renown future ahead of him but was distracted. Twice he had been threatened. Twice he'd had to protect himself. It was pointless to dwell on actions he had been forced to take. What was done was done, but memories were teasing.

After so many years, why was he thinking about Patricia? She had never meant anything to him, just a lustful college encounter. He couldn't envision her face or the color of her hair, but he could hear an echo of a plaintive voice claiming birth control hadn't worked. She had pleaded with him to marry her. If he wouldn't, she needed money or she would have to file a paternity suit. He shouldn't have laughed, but he did and told her his net worth was the ten dollars and loose change he had in his pocket. Her rich Yale lover was a pauper on a scholarship. In a sudden tantrum, she threatened to go public. She would claim rape, and blacken his character so much that the university might withdraw the scholarship. Perhaps, she couldn't have succeeded, but she was toying with his life.

He remembered the moment when icy panic had given way to hot anger. Memory faded until he saw himself holding a long-bladed kitchen knife. Patricia was lying on the floor of her apartment, a halo of blood slowly seeping around her. He was holding bloody hands under the kitchen faucet. He remembered that clearly and knew that must have been when he removed his ring.

When he returned to the dorm, he blurted out everything that had happened to his best friend. Bart had taken over and gone to Patricia's apartment. He collected the knife and several beer cans and disposed of them in a dumpster. He said he hadn't found the ring, but it was never mentioned on the news. If the police had found it, the engraved initials would have traced it back to him, and that hadn't happened.

Q always suspected Bart had the ring. Until recently, it hadn't mattered. When the police questioned Q as one of Patricia's friends, Bart had been his alibi. By lying and tampering with evidence, he had made himself an accessory to murder. He could never change his story—-not until now. What a fool Bart had been to spread his cards.

The wind was blowing harder. Q's memories were more annoying. He tried to force them out of mind. Taking a last glance in the direction of his yacht, he went inside and closed the sliding glass door.

The huge, antique desk he had bought at an estate sale dominated the room he thought of as his home office. Too big for his official office, it had been nicked and battered when he found it. Restored to its former grandeur, it provided the sense of dignity he required. When he wanted to impress, he scheduled meetings here.

He sat down, his leather swivel chair especially made. Leaning forward, he was able to see a sliver of lake. He stared out at it, still trying to clear his mind. Patricia belonged to a distant past. Thinking about her didn't make sense, but Bart was fresh. The more he tried to forget, the more vivid the recollection. It played over in his mind from the moment he realized he had to eliminate Bart's threat.

After rejecting several ideas as too risky, he had thought about the neighborhood where he grew up. If he remembered correctly, Humboldt Park's recreation center was large enough to have storage rooms or secluded nooks. He had decided it was worth checking out. After his razor had lain untouched for several days, he put on clothes he'd picked up at a charity drop off. His housekeeper was startled when he asked to borrow her old car.

The drive had taken him down streets he remembered from boyhood: *Western Avenue, Division Street, California Avenue.* He had always known the old neighborhood wasn't where he belonged. He would never be one in that crowd.

He parked a block from the recreation center and entering had been hit by a pungent, gymnasium odor. The straggly crowd hanging around was a mixture of young and old. A couple of guys down on their luck wouldn't grab much attention. A silencer would keep a gunshot from being heard, especially amid the general din and ruckus of the basketball and handball courts.

Walking upstairs and past the "No Admittance" sign, he had opened the door to a storage room filled with balls and assorted gym equipment. He had waited an hour. No one had come. It was a suitable place. If anyone was nearby when he had his appointment with Bart, he would have to oblige one more time and work out another plan.

He had known choosing a public building had its risks, but Bart might have been suspicious if he had suggested meeting somewhere secluded. As it was, during their phone conversation, Bart sounded dubious.

"Dress in old clothes? Why do we need cloak and dagger stuff all of a sudden?"

"Bart, I have to be careful. The media are scrutinizing every-thing I do and everyone I have contact with. We can't risk a smart ass reporter getting nosey and poking around." He had laughed and said, "At the Humboldt Park recreation center, a couple of Yale bums will go unnoticed."

The following afternoon, Q had returned to the center. Bart was already waiting. He had a bright, red bandana around his neck. Always clothes conscious, Bart must have thought they were posing as down-on-their-luck cowboys.

Despite the bandana, Q had been sure they wouldn't make an impression. With a surreptitious nod, he let Bart know to fol-low him up the stairs, past the *No Admittance* sign, and into the storeroom.

No one in sight.

Q had waited for Bart to enter, then followed him inside. He left the door open, no point in making Bart nervous. Without counting, Bart stuffed the bills Q handed him into his wallet. "I appreciate this. I don't know if you'll believe it, but I intend to pay back everything I owe you when the deal I'm working on comes through."

Q hadn't believed it and was sure he himself was the deal. Bart's requests for loans had never been exorbitant. This time he had asked for more, surely a prelude to what he thought his rea-sonableness had earned him in light of the new situation.

Q had checked the hall one more time.

Bart's laugh had sounded nervous. "When I made that crack about doing my civic duty and writing a book, you know I didn't mean it. I was just being dumb."

Very dumb. Q closed the door. The gun felt heavy in his hand. "Hey, what are you—"

A roar come up from the basketball court. It was the moment. Q aimed at the heart. He watched Bart go down and saw the blood. A large ball dislodged from somewhere. It rolled toward the hand that still held a wallet. Q pulled the wallet away, surprised that in death the fingers had grasped it tight. The dead hand fell atop the ball.

Q had the irrelevant thought that the bandana looked like a noose. More meaningful was the thought that Barton Corbin could never do his civic duty. Taking a last look, Q regretted that, for the second time, he had been forced to take a life.

Q was not a murderer. He was an honorable man with an impeccable reputation. What he had done, he'd had to do, A quick walk to where he had parked his housekeeper's car, a swift change of jacket and shoes, and it would be over forever.

Head down, the brim of his hat pulled low, he had headed across the wide park lawn. Preoccupied, he never saw the man until he bumped into him. Jerking his head up, he'd had an intimate look. More than the rugged face, the thick, snow white hair triggered a memory.

"Snowball?" It was a quick reaction. He was still furious at himself for calling out the name.

"Q, wait!"

Running and trying to shield his face with his arm, he'd heard Snowball call after him. He had been certain no one would recognize him. Someone had. If Snowball—-Q tried for the man's name, Nick maybe--went public and claimed he had been in the park where Bart's body was found, some reporter might try for a Pulitzer by digging for a possible connection. Both in the same Yale graduating class, that would be the place to start. Enough digging might turn up Patricia's name.

Q had decided that if Snowball blabbed and anyone had the audacity to question him about being in the park, a condescending denial would be sufficient. He never lost his confidence. Nothing could ever stand in his way, but until he had read the newspaper on his desk, he hadn't felt completely safe.

He read it again, an insignificant article on a back page: *Arraigned, Leonard Arnold Wilson and Fedrico Haldero for the murder of Barton Corbin.*

Murder during a robbery would get them life without parole unless they went up before an incompetent judge. Haldero had shouted out his innocence, but Wilson had seemed eager to confess.

Wilson's confession pleased Q. It meant that both of them were undoubtedly guilty of other crimes. It didn't matter what crimes convicted them. They deserved their punishment, and the Barton Corbin murder case was closed. Q folded the paper neatly before dropping it into the carved wooden waste basket.

His young assistant tapped on the door.

"What is it?" Saying only three words, Q knew his voice was commanding.

"Your Honor, members of the media are here for your interview and photo shoot."

Judge Mark Quincy Mayfield, newly appointed justice of the Supreme Court, slipped into his robe. In photos he would look very dignified sitting at his impressive desk.

CHAPTER 30

Charlene's plan began to hatch as soon as her father told her he would be in court all day. "Charlene," he had whispered, opening her bedroom door, "are you awake?"

"Daddy, I'm awake," she said, throwing back the covers and sitting up.

He sat on the edge of her bed. "How's it going with you and--"

"My new cousin?" she said, finishing for him. "I'm having a great time."

"Does she talk about herself? Tell you about her background, where she went to school, that sort of thing?"

Charlene shook her head. "I don't even know if she has a boyfriend."

"What *do* you talk about?"

"She asks questions about Uncle Philip. I told her she would have loved Nana and Grandpa Rockcastle. She seems a little inexperienced. I'm showing her around."

"Uncle Philip is glad she's spending time with you, but she's not your responsibility. Don't let her help you get into mischief."

"Daddy, please! I can get into mischief all on my own."

Standing up, he kissed the top of her head. "That's what I'm afraid of. I'll be in court all day, but your mother will be here if anything comes up."

"What do you think might come up?"

"I don't know. That's what worries me."

Watching him leave, Charlene wondered how he would react if he knew she was determined to investigate a murder. She'd had a hard time falling asleep, thinking about it.

If Nick Crane had actually seen a murderer fleeing from his crime, there had to be evidence. How exciting it would be to find the evidence, free two men Uncle Philip thought were innocent, and bring the real murderer to justice. With most of her friends away at college, she didn't have much to do, and solving a murder would be fun. Her cousin would be in on it. They would go at it together, but she would keep the idea to herself until she had a plan.

"Cousin," she called, pounding on the guest room door, "let's get a quick breakfast and go for a drive."

A glass of milk and a muffin were all she wanted and watched impatiently as her cousin ate, silently thinking it shouldn't take so long to finish one boiled egg and two pieces of toast. Finally heading to the car, Charlene offered to let Dominique drive her Camaro.

"It's such a nice car and such a pretty blue. I can't believe you'd let me drive it."

Charlene held out the keys. "Dad keeps it well insured."

Dominique looked away. "I don't have a license."

If Daddy wanted to know something personal about Dominique, Charlene could tell him she didn't drive. She might try a sly approach to finding out the boyfriend status. Better yet, she would just ask.

Traffic was heavy on Outer Drive. Charlene delayed questions until they reached their exit. "The guy I dated during the summer is in his second year at Cornell. I thought I would miss him when he went back, but with you to pal with, I can't say that I do. What's up with you in the romance department?"

"Romance," Dominique repeated. "Nothing is up with me."

"Just as well," Charlene said. "If you don't have anyone special to go back to, it means we can keep you here longer."

"I wish," Dominique said softly, "I could stay here forever."

She sounded sad, and Charlene said, "I'm sure Uncle Philip would like that. We'll stop and see him on the way back."

"Back from where?"

` "You'll see," Charlene said, enjoying being mysterious. She parked in a public garage. After they walked two blocks in combat with the wind, she led Dominique into the lobby of an impressive building.

"What are we going to do here?"

"Visit Daddy's office."

"Didn't your mother remind you that he would be in court all day?"

"That's the idea. Come on. It's on the tenth floor."

Miss Bancroft was at her desk, as poised as ever. Not even Charlene's physical education teacher sat that straight. When introduced to Dominique, she stood and held out her hand. "I heard about you, and I'm so happy for you and your father." For once her smile looked like the real thing.

"Is Daddy busy?" Charlene asked.

"Your father will be in court all day."

"Oh, my," Charlene said, utterly surprised. "I guess he can't take us out for lunch later. Will it be okay for me to show my cousin the view?"

Before Miss Bancroft could answer, Charlene ushered Dominique inside the inner office and closed the door. "Cousin, open the blinds and look out the window," she said, hurrying behind the desk. Nothing looked promising, just the intercom, phone, and a tidy pile of mail in the in-basket.

"What's that place down there on the left? And that fountain! It's beautiful."

"That's the Buckingham Fountain, and the building is the Art Institute."

With her cousin preoccupied, Charlene started searching. Everything looked much too neat. She didn't dare rifle through papers and risk leaving tell-tale disarray. Deciding the phone index might yield something, she flipped it open and ran her finger down the names on the speed dial.

Dominique asked another question, but Charlene's attention was too riveted to answer: *Jerry Finlay, P.I.*

P.I. had to stand for private investigator. Daddy had said he had his investigator looking into the case Uncle Philip was worried about. Unless Daddy used more than one investigator, this had to be the guy. She said the name aloud, took a deep breath, and pressed the number. After several rings, she heard a gruff, "Finlay."

"Good morning," she said, squeezing her nostrils together to mimic Miss Bancroft's voice. "This is Mr. Rockcastle's secretary. He's in court today and asked me to find out if you have additional information about the murder case."

"The Bart Corbin case? I thought he took me off that."

"He took you off the case?" Charlene was surprised and didn't know how to continue. Fortunately, Jerry Finlay, P.I. didn't need coaxing.

"Tell your boss I'm glad he's still interested. It looks like those two guys might be standing in for someone Bart Corbin was putting the screws on. Something happened a long time ago, and there has to have been a major development recently."

Charlene snatched up a pen and began scribbling on a note pad. Finlay talked so fast, it was hard to get it all down: *Bart Corbin, graduated from Yale, has a Yale ring, M.O.M not his initials, old newspaper article about a murder.*

"Wow!" This was terrific stuff, and the word slipped out.

Silence. Then, very slowly, Jerry Finlay, P.I., said, "Who are you?"

Charlene's fingers went back to her nose. "I told you. I'm Miss Bancroft. Mr. Rockcastle's secretary."

"Something's wrong. What's going on?"

"Mr. Finlay, if you're in doubt, I'll hang up and you can call me back."

Slamming down the phone, Charlene dashed to the reception desk. "Miss Bancroft, I'm expecting an important phone call from my boyfriend at Cornell. Let me take it in Daddy's office."

Miss Bancroft looked startled. "Why would he call you here?"

The phone was ringing, no time for a brilliant explanation. "I'm sure that's him. Please, let me take it in Daddy's office."

Carefully closing the door behind her, Charlene dashed back to the desk and picked up the phone. "Mr. Rockcastle's office."

"Did I just talk--"

"Ah, Mr. Finlay! You were talking about your investigation into the Bart Corbin case," she said, properly nasal.

"I'll phone you before I fax a report over, same as always. Now that I know Rockcastle is still interested, I'll stay on it. Did he get my fax about the Kolchek girl? I think he's wrong about her age. She's only eighteen. Several people recognized her from the photo, but the high school she said she attended has no record of her. A neighbor said Jill Kolchek didn't go to high school."

Baffled, Charlene forgot to sound nasal. "Jill Kolchek didn't go to high school. What are you talking about?"

"Hey, something's wrong. What's going on?"

"Nothing's wrong," Charlene said in her nasal best. "I just didn't realize which assignment you were talking about." She said a quick good-bye and snatched up her notes.

Her cousin stared at her, a strange expression on her face. "Why did you say my name?"

"It's not your name anymore. Uncle Philip asked Dad to apply for a court order to have your name changed on all your records."

"Why did you say my name?" she repeated.

Charlene shrugged. "I was talking to an investigator. I suppose Dad has him locating your records for the court order. It's nothing to worry about."

"Yes, it is." Covering her face with her hands, the anger melted. Dominique burst into tears.

"If there's a problem, I'm sure Uncle Philip will understand," Charlene said. She tried to put an arm around her but was pushed away.

"It's not a problem, not exactly. It's just...something."

Charlene whispered, "Cousin, just what?"

"It's what you said. I never went to high school. Mom needed me. I had to stay home. We tried home schooling. Didn't get far with it. Could never go anywhere, do anything—except smoke." She talked in broken sentences. Her voice caught on a sob.

This time she didn't resist when Charlene put an arm around her. "I'm sorry you couldn't go to high school. It's sad, but it wasn't your fault."

"The Rockcastles you told me about all sound so wonderful. I don't think Father Rockcastle would want me for his daughter if he knew I barely finished eighth grade. I could never fit in."

If there were tears in Charlene's eyes, she wouldn't let them fall. "You are a Rockcastle and my cousin," she said proudly. "You're *in* already. You were always one of us."

"Please don't tell...my dad I didn't go to high school. I'm so ashamed."

There was a knock and Miss Bancroft peeked in. "Can I do anything to help?"

Charlene knew she meant, *"Why are you in here so long?"*

"Miss Bancroft, the view still takes my breath away, but we can't spend the whole day looking out the window.

Come on, Dominique. Let's go."

In the elevator, Dominique's tears had stopped, but she still looked shattered. It wouldn't help to say it wasn't as if she had ditched school to hang out with friends. She had been forced to stay home, but her embarrassment couldn't be reasoned away. Charlene had to get her mind on something else.

"I have something to tell you."

She hadn't planned to let Dominique know they were destined to be girl detectives until she worked out a plan, but it was distraction time. "You and I are going to investigate a murder. Won't that be exciting?"

Instead of the eager response Charlene expected, Dominique barely looked up.

"What do you say? I mean, it's not every day that we get a chance to be detectives."

"I don't know anything about being a detective," Dominique said. Softly, she added, "I kind of doubt that you do."

"Of course, I do! CSI is my favorite program. We'll have to watch it together. Meantime, we can get started."

"Started on what?"

"Solving our case." Walking down Michigan Avenue, Charlene explained her plan, or at least as far as she had gotten with it. Details could be worked out later. "We know," she began grandly, "that our victim graduated from Yale."

Dominique said. "He's not our victim."

Her cousin's attitude wasn't what Charlene expected. Probably a few details would bring her around. "If the murdered man went to Yale, maybe the killer did, too."

"Yale has to be a big school or I would never have heard of it. Mom and I watched soap operas all day," Dominique said.

"What we're doing is more exciting than soap operas.

Our victim," Charlene said, stressing the *our*, "had a newspaper article about a murder that happened a long time ago."

"Aren't we going back to the car? It's getting cold."

They were standing on a corner waiting for the light to change. Charlene tried not to sound exasperated. "Don't you get it? Bart Corbin knew the murderer's identity and was killed so he couldn't tell."

"If the murder happened a long time ago, maybe it was solved a long time ago."

Charlene was startled. This was something she hadn't thought of.

Dominique tugged her sleeve. "It's green."

Hustling across the broad street, Charlene had time to reevaluate. "I have a hunch it wasn't solved. My detective's instinct, I guess. We just have to figure out the rest of it."

"The rest of what?"

"We have to find out when Mr. Corbin attended Yale. Then we have to check all his classmates with the initials M.O.M."

"Check all his classmates," Dominique repeated, then started to laugh.

Charlene had wanted to cheer her up, but not this way. "Yes," she said, slightly indignant. "First, we find out when Bart Corbin graduated, then we get a list of everyone who was enrolled in Yale that year."

"How could we do that?"

Charles was stumped. She would have to think of something else.

CHAPTER 31

Philip's mind wandered to the first time he had kissed Susanna. That kiss had changed his life. Now, there had been another first kiss. He wouldn't let that kiss change anything. It was time to put it out of mind and get to work. Sitting at his desk, he shuffled through several days' accumulation of mail.

He opened a business letter requesting information about someone who had listed him as a reference. He didn't recognize the name but would check the church registry.

Despite trying to focus, his thoughts kept drifting to their restaurant sojourn. His gang had been impressively dignified while they ate, but driving home, Charlene had stirred up a little chaos with a quip about silly little boys. When Derek retorted in kind, there had been a burst of cheerful teasing. It had pleased Philip to hear Derek hold his own, but his Dominique never joined in.

He had been headed toward Tara's house until Charlene said, "Uncle Philip, take us to the rectory first. We'll wait there while you take Tara and these two funny characters home."

Dropping the girls off first hadn't been his idea. He assured himself of that. He wondered if Charlene had suspected something.

Turning on the computer, he brought up the registry. The man's unusual last name appeared but with a different first name. "Probably the same family. Good people," he told himself and ran Xs down the excellent column of the query.

He could have dropped Tara and the boys off in front of the house, but he didn't. Carrying Styrofoam boxes of left-overs, he had followed them upstairs. They had been laughing, the conclusion to a refreshing evening.

Putting the boxes in the refrigerator, Tara had chased David and Derek into the living room. "You can watch TV until bedtime," she had said.

Alone together, she had apologized for bringing up the arraignment. "Here I am mentioning it again. I don't know what's the matter with me. Just nervous, I guess."

He hadn't asked why she was nervous. He knew and knew he should leave immediately. He was almost out the door when she said a soft, "Philip." When he turned, she moved toward him. "It was a wonderful evening." She paused. "And you're wonderful, too."

Her arms had slipped around his neck. She raised herself to press her lips to his. Abruptly, she had pulled back. "I'm sorry. Forgive me."

Without thinking, without planning, he grasped her tight, pulling her body close to his. His deep, almost guttural, gasp confirmed it was something he had yearned to do. He had kissed her, not passionately, just enough to feel the warmth of her lips. He caught a whiff of her fragrance, the scent of her hair. For a moment beyond time, he had held her.

She had pulled away. "This is my fault. Please don't be angry."

He had caught her hand, held it to his lips, and kissed it. Her hand had felt small in his, gentle, and somehow in need of his protection. Their eyes locked. *The boys could be sent to bed. They would be alone.*

It had been up to him. He couldn't waver. Without a word, he bolted out the door and took the stairs two at a time.

Philip shoved the reference query in the return envelope and tried to concentrate on sorting the rest of the mail. He noticed the folded yellow paper: *To Whom It May Concern.* It was the letter the girls had given him when he returned to the rectory.

He wasn't sure whether it was his own awareness or whether Charlene really had a knowing little smile when she mentioned Tara. Could she have picked up on something? Charles had said she could be too smart for her own good. He wondered if she was too smart for *his* good.

He set Nick Baker's letter aside. It could wait. For the hundredth time he reached for the phone. He would call Tara and tell her what happened had been an innocent reaction to the laughter and wine. For the hundredth time, he couldn't do it.

The doorbell rang, and he glanced at his calendar. Nothing was scheduled. If someone had a problem that couldn't wait, it might pull his attention off his own dilemma, not that it was a dilemma. He was a priest. There was nothing to decide, no choice to make.

"Uncle Philip, it's us!"

Charlene looked her usual boisterous self, but Dominique looked depressed and hardly glanced up when he greeted her.

As he ushered them into the living room, Charlene was already describing plans she had for showing Dominique the city. "Leave it to me. I'm going to take her on a real tour, not one that just takes you to the touristy stuff."

"Hey, there are places in this city where you shouldn't take her or go yourself. Sticking to the tourist attractions is a good idea."

Charlene laughed. "Good ideas are usually boring. Don't worry, Uncle Philip. I'll never let anything happen to my cousin."

Philip felt an odd apprehension. Something in her voice, in her words, made him uneasy. He shook it off. Charlene was daring, but she would never do anything to put herself or Dominique in real danger.

Dominique hadn't said a word, not even hello, and he put his arm around her. "Dominique, is something wrong?"

She shook her head. "I'm just tired."

"Is Charlene running you around too much?" Philip asked, doubting that was the problem.

He had something planned for when he and Dominique were alone, but maybe it was needed now. Dashing upstairs, he returned carrying a wooden chest. Easing down on the couch between the girls, he lifted the lid. Carefully selecting several pictures, he handed one to Dominique and another to Charlene.

Susanna's daughter stared at her face for the first time. "Her name was Susanna," Philip said, a catch in his voice. "She was your mother."

"Uncle Philip, Mom told me how pretty she was. Dad said she was feisty. You can see that in her picture, too. Cousin, you look like her."

Dominique moaned, "It's not fair. It's not right."

Thinking he understood, Philip said, "The love you felt for the mother who raised you will never die. She was your mom, and that bond is sacred."

Unexpectedly, Dominique lashed out, "You don't understand. When she died, I felt sad, but I was sick of staying home with soap operas playing all day and never going out, except to push a wheelchair. Maybe, she didn't want to be, but she was always angry. She never allowed me to do anything on my own. I was trapped."

Starting to sound hysterical, she stood up. He couldn't interrupt her. It all had to come out. Even Charlene knew to be quiet.

"When I told you she was dead, I cried because I realized how glad I was. I shouldn't feel that way. I know I shouldn't, but I do. Do you hear that? I'm glad my mother is dead."

Philip wanted to say something. A priest, he knew comforting words, but they seemed trite, meaningless. He couldn't use them to comfort his daughter.

Dominique still held Susanna's picture. In a calmer voice, she said, "I wonder what it would have been like if she had been the mother I knew."

Philip wondered, too. When she told him her mother was dead, her tears had been a comfort. Susanna's daughter and the woman she called Mom had known a loving relationship. Until now, his regrets had been for himself because he hadn't had the blessing of raising her. The truth was far more painful. His daughter, Susanna's daughter, had endured a miserable childhood.

"Cousin, you're a Rockcastle now. It doesn't matter that you didn't get to do a lot of things or go to high school. We'll make up for lost time."

"What does she mean, you didn't attend high school? It's the law."

Dominique dropped back on the couch. "The law," she said, sarcastic. "Mom needed me, so I was allowed to be home schooled—-or that's what it was supposed to be."

She took another picture out of the chest. "That's you," she said, "and this is my mother."

Philip watched her trace the outline of Susanna's face with her finger. She had called her *my mother*. She knew her mother's name and what she had looked like. That was soothing, but nothing could undo their daughter's past.

He remembered all the young people he had counseled to stay in school. Several had invited him to their graduations, not so much for his attendance, but to let him know they had stuck it out. Philip was proud of his invitations and the senders who walked across the stage to receive a diploma. Why hadn't his daughter had that opportunity? Why had she been deprived? Confused, he had an eerie awareness. Instead of being angry, he almost felt like laughing at himself.

Charlene announced she was going to the kitchen to raid the refrigerator. Good luck to her! She wasn't going to find much, but he suspected her real intent was to give them time alone. He used it to tell his daughter how much he regretted all she had endured, but he was careful not to sound maudlin. God had reunited them. Philip could devote himself to making her future more fulfilling than her past.

He sat next to her, their shoulders touching, and they sorted through precious pictures of Susanna.

"What's that?" Dominique asked, pointing at something in the box.

Philip lifted out a small doll with a large yellow bonnet. "I bought this for you the day you were born. You were too little to play with it then and you're too old to play with it now."

"I'm not too old to keep it." She took it out of his hand and pressed it to her chest. "Dad, thank you."

Charlene peeked in, checking. He nodded to let her know it was safe.

After the girls left, Philip sat for a long time, the chest on his lap. He tried to think, tried to pray, but he couldn't. Nothing made sense.

When the phone rang, he made no move to answer. Let it ring. The answering machine picked-up and a shaky voice murmured, "This is Rose Deato. Please, Father, please call as soon as you can." A name and number followed, then another *please*.

Please three times in one short sentence, but he didn't reach for the phone. He had never failed to respond to a call like that, but he didn't have the heart to help anyone.

On the day Dominique was born, he had cradled her in his arms. Without planning, without thinking, he had sprinkled water on her forehead. He had performed the holy rite because his daughter would be called home before her formal baptism. The thought had been a beautiful comfort, but it wasn't true. She hadn't been called home. She had lived to endure years of unhappiness.

Restless, he went for a long drive. He felt confused and adrift. It was very late when he parked the car and went up the stairs. He gave the door a light tap with his knuckle.

"Who is it?"

"Tara, it's me."

CHAPTER 32

When Charlene awoke the next morning, she stretched, laced her fingers behind her head, and gazed at the ceiling. Staying in bed late was one of her favorite exercises. With no classes to attend, she could indulge. She would soon have to submit an application to a college for next year's enrollment. Notre Dame had been Daddy's idea and a big bore. Now, he was inundating her with information about other schools he thought were suitable. Smiling to herself, she stretched again. This time, she would choose. It would be a school that specialized in one of her particular interests.

She had earned praise and A's in her high school journalism class and had discovered a real knack for interviewing people. Life as a reporter-at-large for a major publication could be exciting. She had a great sense of style and had considered the fashion industry. Becoming an actor was also considered. She knew from experience that she could give very convincing performances when the need arose.

With so many options, she hadn't been able to make up her mind, but the dilemma was resolved. She would find a college that would train her to be a detective. Actually, she already was a detective and hard at work on her first case. Thinking about it gave her the motivation to abandon the bed and get dressed. On the phone, she wouldn't be seen, but it would be hard playing the part wearing pajamas.

As a graduation gift, she had refurbished her bedroom and replaced the Tinker Bell motif writing table with a fashionable desk. She sat at the desk as rigidly straight as Miss Bancroft and, after a few deep breaths to put herself in character, dialed Mr. Finlay's number. Imitating Miss Bancroft's voice was no longer a challenge. She was confident he would never doubt Daddy's secretary was on the line.

"Mr. Finlay, I'm calling for Mr. Rockcastle," she said to the now familiar gruff voice that answered. "He'll be in court again today. He's concerned that he hasn't received your report on the Corbin case."

"Miss Bancroft, I gave you an update on the phone. I faxed a complete report."

She didn't wait for him to finish. "Perhaps," she said, "but Mr. Rockcastle has questions about some of the details."

"What does he need?"

"Regarding the newspaper article about a murder, it will help if he knows the name of the victim."

"I'll send a report later."

"No." she said, for once speaking before clearing her throat. "Mr. Rockcastle needs the name of the murder victim." Softer, she said, "He suspects the murder was never solved."

"The name I'm coming up with for the murder victim is Pam. No, not Pam, Pat. The name was Patricia Lazarus. I think this Lazarus stayed dead."

"Huh? What do you mean 'stayed dead'?"

"Never mind," he said. "I don't think the Lazarus murder was solved. Corbin must have had information the murderer was afraid of."

"That's exactly what I think," the knockoff Miss Bancroft said. He had told her what she wanted to know and gave him a crisp goodbye.

Turning on her computer, she created a new file: *The Bart Corbin Murder Case*

She intended to keep careful records of all her cases and perhaps write a book, but that could come later. She typed quickly. When she was finished, she needed two things-—her cousin to listen to what she had written and something to eat.

In the kitchen, she ignored the assortment of food in the refrigerator and slipped a piece of cheese between two slices of bread. It wasn't necessarily breakfast fare, but she could carry it while looking for her cousin, not that Dominique would be hard to find.

Not allowed to smoke indoors, she usually did her smoking on the sprawling patio that circled the rear of the house. The long expanse of backyard led down to the lake. Today, big waves were churning. The air had a mean snap. Dominique was huddled on the stairs leading down to the yard. One hand was deep in the pocket of a green, corduroy jacket, the other held a cigarette. She was wearing the clothes she'd had on the night she came. They were a long way from new and had never been stylish. Charlene was struck by how forlorn she looked.

"Please, Cousin, it's too cold for you out here. I have something that will cheer you up, and you're involved in it."

Dominique took another deep puff before looking up.

"In what?"

"The Bart Corbin murder case. You're going to help me solve it."

Dominique shrugged. "It's already been solved. Two guys are in jail. The police won't investigate it anymore."

"That's my point. It's up to us to catch the real killer and free two innocent men."

"How do you know the guys in jail aren't the killers? The police must know what they're doing."

This wasn't the reaction Charlene had hoped for, but she would bring her cousin around. "I have everything written down. Come on. I'll explain it to you."

Charlene finished her sandwich and picked up a doughnut on her way to her bedroom. She pointed her cousin to her room's only arm chair and cleared her throat. "I'll start at the beginning."

"The beginning of what?"

Dominique was clearly a witness for the opposition, but that was good. Before a court case, Daddy sometimes rehearsed his presentation with a legal assistant whose job was to attack weak points. It helped him strengthen his case, and her cousin would help strengthen hers.

She kept her voice formal. "According to Mr. Nick Crane, the man who brought a letter to the rectory--"

"I told you, he's a troublemaker."

"Perhaps." Stiffening, Charlene half-closed her eyes. "That doesn't mean he didn't know what he was talking about."

"He didn't talk about anything. He just left that letter."

This was going nowhere fast and was not what Charlene had planned. "Listen to me!" she said, trying not to sound exasperated. "I talked to that detective again. Mr. Finlay thinks Barton Corbin was trying to blackmail the man who killed him. There was another murder a long time ago. Barton Corbin must have been the bad guy's alibi and was trying to blackmail him."

Dominique interrupted. "If this murder happened a long time ago, why was Barton Corbin blackmailing him now?"

"Mr. Finlay said Corbin talked about having to do his civic duty. If he was talking to the murderer, it might mean that his killer had won the lottery or something. That would have changed the situation."

"Maybe," Dominique said, "but if Corbin had lied, wouldn't he be in trouble if now he told the truth?"

Charlene thought that over. "There's something called a statute of limitations. I don't know how long it lasts for giving false information."

Her cousin frowned. "If Corbin said he would do his civic duty, he must have thought the guy he protected was going to commit another crime, like something that would hurt people. I don't think it could be for anything like winning the lottery."

Her cousin made sense. Impressed, Charlene turned back to her notes. "I think we could figure out the name if we could get hold of Mr. Crane's letter."

As she said the words, they convinced her. "That's it! We'll go to the rectory. While you're talking to Uncle Philip, I can look in his office. Yellow paper will be easy to spot."

"No! I won't let you search my dad's office, and I don't think we should talk to Nick Crane."

Charlene wasn't deterred. This was her first case, and she would solve it. Before she could tell her cousin her newest idea, she heard the downstairs phone. Her mother called up the stairs, "Dominique!"

Running down the stairs, Dominique called over her shoulder. "I don't think we should try to solve a murder. It could be dangerous."

CHAPTER 33

Philip was usually totally focused when he celebrated Mass, but this morning, his mind wandered. Last night, he had broken a vow. His guilt was more intellectual than emotional. His emotion was for Tara. She was in love with him. Despite all his resolves, he had let their relationship cross the line. More than anything else, he didn't want her to be hurt.

After Susanna died, more than one woman made it clear she was available. He wasn't. He couldn't taint the love he had shared with Susanna by casually falling into bed with someone with a beckoning finger. Later, when he decided to return to the seminary, he was grateful he hadn't responded to subtle and not so subtle offers.

It was different with Tara. Although she re-ignited a passion he had persuaded himself he'd suppressed, his desire for her went far beyond the physical. In some uncanny way, they blended. There were times when he thought she was reading his mind, but one night of lovemaking couldn't change his situation.

When Mass was over, he brushed off Don's attempt at conversation. At home, he put on his jogging suit but, instead of going for a run, he went to his office. Lounging back in his chair, he put his feet on the desk.

Life had been predictable, not easy perhaps, but he had known who he was and what he thought. Lately, life was a confusion and coming at him fast. It had begun with Leonard. His ill-advised attempts to help a sick mind had resulted in a psychotic confession and two innocent men indicted for murder. Despite all his assurances to Rico Haldero's mother, there was nothing he could do.

Discovering he had a living daughter was the most glorious thing that ever happened to him, but it came at a price. After the accident, he had comforted himself with the conviction that it had been God's will. Now, he knew they had been separated by a mistake and a deliberate deception.

It tortured him to know their precious Dominique had been deprived, not only of school attendance, but also of normal teenage activities. He suspected she had taken up smoking because it was one of the few things she could do on her own.

Was he using regrets about his daughter's hardships to justify his behavior?

At the thought, Philip jerked to his feet. He was thinking in circles and needed a run to clear his mind. Heading for the door, he heard the phone and let the answering machine pick it up: "Father Rockcastle, this is Avery Upton again, calling from *Greet Today's Faces*, to invite you and your daughter to appear on our program."

She continued, repeating what she had said in an earlier message. Philip hadn't responded. He had no desire to tell his story on television but, as Upton repeated what they were offering, he reconsidered.

"We will fly you and your daughter to New York first class and put you up in an excellent hotel. You will have an expense account for meals and, of course, you will be paid."

There wasn't much in a financial way Philip could do for his daughter. As Avery Upton was giving her number, he picked up the phone.

"This is Father Rockcastle."

They talked for some time, and Philip was intrigued. A trip to New York City with Dominique would give them long, private hours together. They could make up for some of the lost years. He envisioned them strolling side by side through Central Park.

He considered something else. "How much will we be paid?"

She quoted a figure. He was impressed and decided it was too much to reject out of hand. "Miss Upton, I assume my daughter will also be paid."

She assured him of it and started talking about dates. "We need to go with it as soon as possible, while your story is still hot."

He drew back. Could he really go on television and answer questions about the most meaningful things in his life?

"It's a talk show, isn't it? Before I agree to anything, I'd have to know what questions I would be asked. My daughter would, too."

"Father Rockcastle, of course, you need to know the questions in advance. If one touches on a topic you would rather not talk about, we'll simply cross it off." She added, "Pictures will be very helpful, especially wedding pictures of you and your daughter's mother."

How could he hold up a picture of Susanna and talk about the accident that killed her? Wavering he said, "I'll let you know. I can't make a commitment until I talk it over with my daughter."

Philip sensed that if he gave himself time to think about it, he would decide not to do it, but Dominique should have a say. Without putting down the receiver, he punched in a number.

"Marge," he said when his sister-in-law answered, "this is Philip. Is Dominique there or are our girls out on the town?"

"Phil, she's upstairs. I'll call her."

He waited, then heard an eager, "Dad." He closed his eyes, still hardly believing every time he heard her say it.

"I was glad when Aunt Marge called me to the phone. You rescued me."

"I rescued you? You have to let me know all about it, but first I want to tell you something. We are invited to be guests on *Greet the Faces*. It's taped in New York, and they would arrange for our flight." He told her everything Avery Upton had said and waited for her reaction.

After a long pause, she asked, "Would they ask me questions? I mean, would they want to know where I went to school and about things that happened to me?"

"Not if we told them not to," he assured her. Her question stabbed but, if his daughter was ashamed of gaps in her education, it was a wrong he resolved to make right. The money they could earn on television would help. "I think we should do it," he said, making up his mind.

"New York City," she said. "I never dreamed I'd get to go there."

"We'll go there together," he told her. "Now, Dominique, tell me how I rescued you."

"I think Charlene wants to keep it secret."

"You'd better not give it away," he said, pleased that his daughter and niece were forming a bond.

"I think, maybe, it would be better if I did tell you. Charlene wants to be a detective and she wants me in on it."

"Indeed!" He tried not to laugh. "What does Charlene have in mind?"

"Two guys are in jail for a murder. She doesn't think they're guilty. It all started with that pesky guy in your class."

"Do you mean Nick Crane?" he said, losing the urge to laugh.

"Yes, he left a letter addressed to *To Whom It May Concern*. When I told Charlene he had tried to talk about a murder, she got interested and decided the letter concerned us. She read it and gave it to me to read. I didn't want to."

"You probably shouldn't have," he said, trying to sound more like a dad than a priest, "but how did I rescue you?"

"Charlene thinks she can find the real murderer and solve the case. She wants us to do it on our own, but I don't think it's a good idea."

Charles had said Charlene was fearless. Philip didn't doubt it and worried she might try something foolish and land herself in trouble. He cautioned Dominique, "Try to keep an eye on her. If anything she does seems risky, let me know. Don't let her talk you into anything."

Before they hung up, he said he would keep her posted on plans for their trip.

His bishop had been adamant about his not going public about his daughter. Going on a talk show was going as public as possible, but their story was already well-known. How else would a talk show know to be interested in them? He would check with the diocese and request a few days vacation. When he had dates, he would get back to Avery Upton.

Meantime, he wondered about what a bright, eighteen-year-old detective with an active imagination might try. He would have to read Nick's letter to see what set her off. The man was no fool and might actually have useful information, but his letter would have to wait. Philip had to make arrangements to take his daughter to New York.

CHAPTER 34

On Saturday morning, Charlene helped her cousin pack for her trip to New York. Far from wishing she was going along, she had exciting plans of her own. When Dominique returned, they would both have stories to share.

"Cousin, use my suitcase. You have to get Uncle Philip to take you shopping, and it will hold a lot."

Dominique's aunt had sent a box of her belongings—-books mostly and some clothes. Their shopping trips had added to her wardrobe but, to Charlene, it was still meager. She scanned her closet. "Take this blue pants suit. You may have to pull the pants up a little high under the top, but it will look great on you and be just right for your TV appearance."

Uncle Philip had planned to pick Dominique up on the way to the airport, but she had persuaded him to let her drive Dominique to the rectory. There had been no point in mentioning it would give her a chance to look for Nick Crane's letter.

When she and her cousin closed the suitcase and carried it downstairs, Daddy was waiting. "I have something for you," he told Dominique and handed her a package. She opened it and took out a framed picture.

"It's your mother." He hesitated. "You can leave it here until you get back. I didn't see it at first, but you remind me of her more every time I look at you. She didn't smoke. She wouldn't want you to smoke." Picking up the suitcase, he led the way to the car.

As Charlene pulled out of the driveway, Dominique said, "If your father thinks I should quit smoking, I wonder why he bought me cigarettes."

"Daddy hates smoking. He lets clients smoke in his office and then ups his fees. When he bought you cigarettes, he was just trying to be kind."

"Or maybe," her cousin said softly, "he didn't think I was really the baby everyone thought was dead. He wanted me to trust him so he could find out the truth."

"He knows who you are now," Charlene said, not interested in a conversation about cigarettes. She was concentrating on how to have time alone in Uncle Philip's office.

At the rectory, Uncle Philip introduced them to the curate who would take his place while he was gone. Charlene was relieved when Uncle Philip took him upstairs to show him his room.

Now was the time. "Quick! Be my lookout," Charlene whispered, tugging Dominique to the door of the office.

"No, it's not right."

"Do it!"

Charlene didn't close the door. Keep everything casual, no point in acting suspicious. The desk looked cluttered. Uncle Philip didn't have a Miss Bancroft to keep everything pristine. So much the better. She didn't have to worry about leaving a telltale mess.

Yellow, look for yellow.

It took only moments to spot Nick Crane's letter amid the pile. She had planned to decipher the crossed-out name, but Dominique was signaling her.

"Hurry! They're coming back."

Quickly scanning the pages, she saw Nick Crane's signature written in bold letters. Under it was a phone number. Six, zero, six—she said the number aloud, memorizing it. She didn't take time to shove the letter back into the pile. If it were still atop the desk when Uncle Philip returned home, he would never connect it to her.

Her goodbyes to her uncle and cousin were sincere but brief. She was eager to get home and phone Mr. Nick Crane. Driving, she considered several personas and decided on Miss Bancroft. True, he wouldn't be familiar with Miss Bancroft's voice, but she did the impersonation so well, it was a shame not to put it to further use.

At home, she lingered in the family room just long enough to seem casual. Her parents weren't apt to wonder what she was planning to do, but a detective should always be cautious.

Upstairs, she sat down at her desk, composed herself, and punched in the number. When a woman answered, Miss Bancroft's impersonator asked, "Is this the residence of Mr. Nick Crane?"

Told that it was, the impersonator said, "I presume I am speaking to Mrs. Crane. If it is convenient, I should like a few words with your husband."

"Who's calling?"

"An associate of Father Rockcastle." She wasn't lying. She was indeed his associate. Better than that, she was his niece.

A masculine voice came on the line. "It's about time he got in touch with me."

He sounded annoyed, but his words assured her he hadn't talked to Uncle Philip. She had been prepared to act as if this were a follow-up call, but that wouldn't be necessary. "Father Rockcastle asked me to contact you. It's in reference to a letter you wrote."

"I expected to hear from him right away. We can't take our time on this. There's more to it than I said in the letter."

"He's been very busy."

"Is he there now?"

"Father Rockcastle is on the way to New York City, but he read your letter before he left. If you answer a few questions, I can give him the information." She waited, expecting him to consent. When he didn't, she had to plunge in.

"You said you encountered someone in the park shortly after Barton Corbin's body was found."

"No," he barked. "It was *before* the body was found."

"Yes, of course," she said getting flustered. "I...I mean Father Rockcastle, understands that both guys...I mean, men, attended Yale. Something happened years ago, possibly when they were at school."

Nick Crane interrupted with a sharp, "I said that in my letter. Corbin must have figured that with his name showing up in the news it was the time to tighten the screws."

"The screws on *who*?" Charlene said, excited.

There was a long silence. Charlene thought they had been disconnected until a soft, much calmer voice asked, "Who are you?"

"Mr. Crane, I told you. I'm an associate of Father Rockcastle."

"What do you mean by associate?"

"Helper," she said quickly.

"Your voice sounds a heck of a lot younger than it did a minute ago. What's going on?"

She forced a laugh. "Everyone tells me that." She was losing ground. Not daring to pause, she continued. "Mr. Crane, tell me the name of the man you saw, and I'll let Father Rockcastle know."

"Hell no. I'm not about to give the name up over the phone." He sounded angrier with every word. "I don't know if anyone will believe it, but I know who I saw. Tell the priest if he wants to help Wilson and Haldero, he can damn well call me himself." She heard the phone slam down.

So much for Miss Bancroft. She had worked once but not twice.

The call had not been a waste. She knew now that the murderer's name had been in the news. It was a promising lead, but she needed more. Miss Bancroft would have to give Mr. Jerry Finlay another call.

CHAPTER 35

As the plane taxied to the runway, Philip clasped a hand over his daughter's clenched fist. It was her first flight. Excitement had given way to anxiety. "Try to relax and enjoy it," he told her. "It's a clear day. Before we land you'll get a great view of the Statue of Liberty."

Boarding, they had attracted a number of quizzical looks. A priest traveling with an attractive young woman was worthy of attention. Perhaps, he should have been concerned that they were fueling negative surmises, but he didn't care. For three days, he would have his daughter almost exclusively to himself. They would have to do the television appearance. With the right attitude, that might be fun. He would devote the rest of the time to getting to know Susanna's daughter.

Whenever he asked her questions and tried to develop a rapport, she pulled back. She was uneasy. He sensed her lack of a high school diploma wasn't the only thing that troubled her. If she would confide in him, he would try to help her. He had missed the first eighteen years of her life and hoped he could still be a supportive dad.

When they exited the plane at JFK, they saw a young woman holding up a sign. "I'm Father Rockcastle," he told her, reading his name.

Smiling and as animated as if she were greeting dear friends, she told them she was from *Greet the Faces* and had a car waiting. Philip was pleased that his daughter was getting VIP treatment.

At the hotel, separate but adjacent rooms were reserved for them. Philip signed the register, then watched enthralled as his daughter wrote *Dominique Rockcastle.* Their rooms were at the end of a long corridor and a distance from the nearest elevator. They might not be the most convenient, but it didn't matter. Dominique was thrilled. "I never saw a room like this," she said. "Look at the bed. I can't believe I'm going to sleep there."

Philip laughed, not at her but at the moment. Accepting the *Greet the Faces* offer had been the right decision. They were already having a time to remember and nothing could spoil it.

After a late dinner in a restaurant their guide recommended, they walked a short distance to Times Square. It was cold, and he turned up the collar on her jacket.

She glanced up at him. "Thanks, Dad." Those two words impressed him more than all the lights on Broadway.

In the morning, they walked to St. Patrick's Cathedral for an early morning Mass. She was awed by St. Patrick's grandeur. He was awed to have her kneeling beside him.

When the church service was over, they rode the subway to the Bowery for a ferry ride to Staten Island.

"What's in Staten Island?" she asked when he told her their destination.

"Dominique, I have no idea, but the ferry goes right by the statue and the view of the city is magnificent."

It was a great start. They played eager tourists for the rest of the day. In the evening, heading back to the hotel, they were too weary for the long conversation Philip had hoped for.

At breakfast, they were paged and told a limousine had arrived to take them to the studio. It was parked in the driveway of the hotel, and the uniformed driver held the door for them. Climbing in, Dominique looked even more scared than she had waiting for the plane to take off.

Philip reassured her. "This should be fun and it won't take more than a few hours. Afterward, we can take a tour or go on a carriage ride in Central Park.

Arriving at the studio, Dominique asked why people were lined up outside. "They're the audience," the driver told her. "They'll start letting them in any minute now."

"The audience," Dominique murmured, slipping down in her seat. "I never thought about that."

"Dominique, where is that brassy girl who stood on my doorstep, demanding to know who I was?"

He heard a soft, "She never existed."

Avery Upton greeted them with a profusion of gratitude and delight. It was a polished act, and Philip hoped it would put Dominique at ease. They were ushered to a large dressing room and told to sit on chairs lined up in front of a long mirror. A woman introduced herself as Sherry and started draping them,

Philip asked, "What's this for?"

"It will keep powder and make-up from getting on your clothes."

"No make-up on me," Philip said, standing up.

Sherry was insistent. "Father, just let me use a touch of powder to keep you from glowing under the lights."

Reluctant, he sat down again and let Sherry apply powder but put his arm up when she came at him with a cosmetic. "Enough," he said.

Sherry had better luck with Dominique. She sat immobile, staring at herself in the mirror as make-up was applied and her hair brushed.

Avery took them to the stage and showed them the entrance where they would walk in. "Miss Clarkson will talk to you before she interviews you on camera."

"I thought you were going to interview us."

"Father, *Greet the Faces* is Lucy Clarkson's show. I'm her assistant."

Philip had seen Lucy Clarkson when he watched several segments of the show before he signed the contract. He had decided the show reached for the maudlin but was not vulgar nor morally objectionable.

One segment he saw featured a couple who had fallen in love as teenagers and rekindled their relationship after a forty-year separation. The moving moment was when the man was presented with a daughter and grandchildren he hadn't known existed. In another segment, a weeping mother told how she'd had to turn her daughter in for drug use because imprisonment was the young woman's only hope of getting clean. The show liked to exploit situations, but Philip wasn't concerned. Their situation had no dark corners.

At Lucy Clarkson's arrival, they went through another round of extra-hearty greetings. She was very slender, and Philip suspected her youthful façade likely reflected the efforts of Sherry or a counterpart. He took her for close to his own age.

She led them to a pleasant room where they chatted. "I want you to be relaxed," she said. "That's the most important thing. When we're on stage, just answer my questions and you'll both do great."

"I'd like to see a list of the questions," Philip said.

Lucy Clarkson smiled. "Avery took notes when she talked to you. Most of my questions will relate to what you told her."

Philip found Lucy easy to like and was grateful to her for putting Dominique at ease. His daughter was smiling when they were signaled to walk on stage where several couches were arranged in studied casualness.

Lucy stood up. "Let's have a special welcome for Father Philip Rockcastle and his precious, long-lost daughter, Dominique."

The applause was thunderous. Philip found it inspiring. His living daughter was a miracle of God, and miracles don't belong under a bushel.

When they were seated, Lucy began telling how Dominique had discovered Father Rockcastle was her father. "They first saw each other when Dominique sat in the front pew of his church during a service. They made eye contact. From that moment had a connection."

That wasn't what Philip had told Avery Upton. He thought the truth was dramatic enough but didn't correct her. Her next comments were harder for him. She told about the accident as he had known she would. He couldn't bring himself to hold up Susanna's picture and handed it to Lucy.

"She's beautiful," Lucy gasped, holding it up for the camera to zoom in. "Dominique, you look so much like her."

Mention of Susanna was over, and Philip sighed inwardly. It hadn't been as heart-wrenching as he had feared.

"Did you enter the seminary immediately after your wife's death?"

"No, Lucy. It was several years before I returned to the seminary."

"Of course, you didn't know you had a living child."

"No, I didn't."

"Would you have returned to the seminary if you had known?"

"Lucy, as the father of a child, I wouldn't have been allowed to return. Certainly, with a little girl to care for, I wouldn't have wanted to."

She asked him a few more questions, then turned her attention to Dominique. "Growing up, you didn't know your real name was Dominique Rockcastle, did you?"

Dominique shook her head.

Smiling, Lucy said, "Dear, speak up. The audience wants to hear you."

"No, I didn't," Dominique said.

"You thought your name was Jill Kolchek."

Philip thought hard. Had he mentioned that name to Avery? He didn't think so and realized they had done some investigating.

"Tell us how it felt to discover your father was a Catholic priest."

Dominique shrugged. "I went to his class. I liked him. I wasn't going to tell him who I was, but somehow I just did."

"Was it a relief to find out that Edward Kolchek wasn't your father?" Without waiting for Dominique's answer, Lucy turned to the audience. "This girl thought her father was in prison for *nasty* crimes and discovers that her real father is a Catholic priest. Isn't that something?"

She had emphasized nasty and the audience responded with gasps as the color drained from Dominique's face.

"We're not going to talk about the ugly crimes Edward Kolchek was convicted of, but it must have been difficult, a young, *innocent* girl living in the house with him," she stressed the word innocent.

Perhaps, not everyone would get it, but Philip did. Edward Kolchek had been convicted of sex crimes. Her *young, innocent girl* remark was to suggest Dominique had been one of his victims. She looked as if she'd been struck across the face.

Philip's impulse was to get up and take her out of there, but the program was live. If he left abruptly, it would underscore Lucy Clarkson's subtle innuendoes.

Lucy Clarkson was not the warm-hearted person she had seemed when she so caringly put them at ease. Her goal was to enthrall her audience, even if it meant mortifying a young girl by hinting that she had been molested. Philip wouldn't let her get away with it.

"Yes, Mr. Edward Kochek is in prison as a result of an embezzlement conviction," he said, staring at Clarkson. "He had expected to replace the money he took but didn't have time. Like many decent men, he made a stupid mistake." They were broadcasting live. He was a Catholic priest. She wouldn't dare contradict him.

"Dominique visited him and told him about me. He's disappointed she's not his daughter, but he still loves her. He asked her to tell me to be a more responsible father than he was." He smiled at Dominique, "I'll do my best."

He had succeeded in flustering Lucy Clarkson. She had been vying for sensationalism--child molestation and probably seeing Dominique break down. He had thwarted her, and she knew it.

Lucy stood up, a signal their interview was over, and thanked them again for coming. Philip whispered to Dominique, "Let the audience see you smile." Like a trouper, she beamed at the audience and the sound of applause followed them down the corridor.

Philip didn't wait to find out if the limousine was available for a ride back to the hotel. Taking her arm, he said, "Let's get out of here."

They walked aimlessly until they came to Central Park. Finding a bench, they sat down. Only then did they talk. "I'm sorry for everything you went through," Philip said, hoping she understood he referred, not to the program, but to the mistreatment. This wasn't the way he wanted to find out, but now he knew what troubled her.

"You understood what she meant. That's why you said what you did about my — I don't want to call him my father. Thank you. It helped a lot."

"I want you to know, really know deep down inside, that nothing that was ever done to you was your fault. I know it, and God knows it."

Her laugh was unexpected. "I'm glad you know it. I'm glad you're my Dad."

CHAPTER 36

Miss Bancroft had failed to trick Nick Crane, but Charlene wasn't finished with her. On Monday, Miss Bancroft would give Mr. Jerry Finlay another call. It was an agonizing wait, but Daddy's secretary wouldn't be working on the weekend.

Charlene carefully wrote out the questions she would ask. At nine o'clock on Monday, she reached for the phone. "Good morning, Mr. Finlay."

"Miss Bancroft," he said, "what's on the agenda?"

She cleared her throat. "Mr. Rockcastle wants to know whether the police solved the murder reported in the newspaper article Barton Corbin saved. Have you been able to research any-thing on that?" Charlene read from her script. Her words as well as her voice had to mimic Miss Bancroft.

"Didn't you get my fax?"

"Mr. Finlay, I don't seem to have it at the moment. In essence, what did it say?" Charlene was pleased with *essence*. It sounded like a word Miss Bancroft would use.

"I got lucky when I phoned the New Haven PD, and wrangled being a retired cop into getting a detective to dig out the Lazarus file. Apparently, she was telling friends she expected to marry into money. Several guys she was known to date were investigated but had solid alibis. Jackson--he's the detective--said he'd get in touch if he came up with anything else."

"He's already come up with a lot," Charlene blurted. "I bet the murderer was one of the men they investigated, and Barton Corbin was his alibi. This is so exciting!"

"You're not Bancroft. Who the hell are you?" blasted in her ear.

Miss Bancroft was dead. Charlene murmured good-bye and hung up. Mr. Finlay would surely contact the prototype. A little investigating would identify the imposter. To stay out of deep trouble, Charlene had to solve the case quickly.

Charlene was close to solving her first case. She didn't have a name, but his initials were MOM, and O, his middle initial, was his nickname. She knew he went to Yale, but that wasn't much to go on. Even if she could find a way to check Yale records, it would take half of forever to track him down that way.

She would get Dominique to deal with Nick Crane. No false identities this time. Her cousin would have to contact him and ask him straight out who it was he saw in the park.

It was an agonizing wait for Dominique to get back from New York. Meantime, Charlene had to stay clear of Daddy. She didn't want him to have a chance to ask if she knew anything about the Bancroft impersonation. If he did ask, she wouldn't lie to him. That was dishonorable. Anyway, she'd never get away with it. Daddy could spot a liar from the back of a courtroom.

Uncle Philip and Dominique came home on Tuesday, but it was Wednesday afternoon before Charlene had a chance to get Dominique alone. They were in her bedroom. Before detailing her plan, she listened to her cousin's eager stories about New York City. They had ridden the ferry past the Statue of Liberty, gone to a play on Broadway, and shopped on Fifth Avenue. She acted vague when Charlene told her how impressed she'd been with her TV appearance, but enough about New York. It was time to get down to business.

Before explaining Dominique's role to her, she brought her up to speed. "What we need to do now," she continued, "is find out who Nick Crane saw. That's your job."

"My job? No way."

"When we catch a murderer and free two innocent men, you'll be glad you helped."

Dominique shook her head. "Hunting for murderers is not a good idea."

Charlene considered guilt-tripping her: *After everything I've tried to do for you...*

She wouldn't stoop to that. Instead, she would talk to Nick Crane herself. The best approach would be to give him a little information to draw him in, but not too much information. This was her case. She didn't want to share the glory. Another phone call impersonation was out. It would have to be face to face.

"Cousin, your dad has his class tonight. Let's go. It'll be fun." Attending a catechism class rated just below dancing with a gorilla, human or simian, on Charlene's list of things to do, but it would give her a chance to meet Nick Crane.

Dominique seemed surprised but not at all reluctant. "My dad hoped I would attend the class again. He said everyone was eager to see me now that they knew who I was." She added softly, "I think he wants to show me off."

Driving to the class, Charlene heard more about New York City. It wasn't boring because most of the time she wasn't listening. Traffic and her murder case bought most of her attention.

They were the first to arrive for the class, and Uncle Philip was delighted. "Dominique, I thought you would have seen enough of me over the weekend," he said, a big grin on his face.

They waited in the office and Charlene looked eagerly at each person who arrived. When Uncle Philip was ready to begin, no one had come who matched Dominique's description of Nick Crane.

"This is a very special night," Uncle Philip began. "I think most of you already know that the young lady who called herself Jane Doe is actually Dominique Rockcastle, my daughter. Sitting next to her this evening is Charlene Rockcastle, my niece."

A woman lunged at Dominique and gave her a big hug. She managed to say, "How wonderful," before bursting into tears.

A young couple pulled their attention away from each other long enough to say hello. Almost everyone seemed delighted, no one more so than Uncle Philip, no one less so than Charlene. If Nick Crane didn't show up, the trip was a real dud.

"I don't usually start this class with a prayer, but tonight is special. Please, let's bow our heads and thank God for the miracle of family."

Crossing herself, Charlene prayed that God would help her discover the killer's name.

An old woman raised a feeble hand. "Father, can we have a prayer for the boy who used to mow my lawn? On television, it said he just came back from Washington where he talked to the Senate about a very important job."

"We can have a prayer for him. What position was being considered?"

"What did you say, Father?"

Uncle Philip shouted. "Mrs. Tobin, what's the job?"

"Oh, yes," she said. "It's a very good job. He was a hard working boy. Everyone was happy for him when he got a scholarship to Yale. He deserved it. His family didn't have money and couldn't have sent him to college."

Uncle Philip looked startled. "His name couldn't be Mayfield, could it? Judge Mayfield?" he shouted.

"Oh yes, Mark Mayfield. He grew up just a few miles from here. On the news, it said he still lives in the city. He's going back to Washington soon to be sworn in as a justice of the Supreme Court."

A young guy sitting behind Charlene let out a gasp. "Wow, a Supreme Court justice."

Everyone had something to say. Even Uncle Philip looked amazed. After the comments ceased, he said, "Let us join in a prayer for Judge Mayfield. Let us ask God to help him be worthy of that high office."

Charlene wasn't in church, but a rectory had to count for something. She didn't get the name she had prayed for, but she heard about Judge Mark Mayfield. He would care that two men from the neighborhood where he grew up were in jail for a murder they didn't commit. The poor victim had gone to Yale, his own school.

Getting the attention of someone so important wouldn't be easy, but two things gave Charlene confidence. As a high school reporter, she had succeeded in getting an interview with the mayor and, if she had heard Judge Mayfield's name in answer to a prayer, she couldn't lose.

He would be going back to Washington soon. She didn't have much time. Her best bet was to introduce herself with a letter, the way she had with the mayor. Granted, a mayor of a big city couldn't be compared to a justice of the Supreme Court, but a letter had worked once. She felt sure it would work again.

At home, she hurried to her room and started composing her letter. Dominique left her alone until midnight when she tapped on the door.

"You're still writing letters? Aunt Marge and I watched a good movie, and I'm going to bed."

Dominique was right. Charlene was writing letters, not *a* letter. In the first one, she tried to include everything she knew about the case. After reading it over, she realized it was too long. It might take too much of his time. The next version was shorter, but it was a struggle to decide which details to include and which to leave out.

It was one o'clock in the morning, and Charlene still hadn't written a letter she thought would work. She was getting sleepy, but a sudden brainstorm brought her awake. Her letter didn't need details. She would write a very short letter and give just enough information to arouse his interest.

CHAPTER 37

*Two men are in jail charged with the murder of Barton Corbin.
The police regard the case as closed, but the men are innocent. I
have proof that Corbin was killed by someone he knew when he
was at Yale. What should I do?*

Charlene didn't sign the letter but ended with her phone number. When she reread it in the morning, she was positive it was the way to go. It gave the basics, and Judge Mayfield could read it in two seconds. She had ended with a question, remembering a writing class tip that recommended ending with a question to involve the reader.

Her envelopes were pale pink and the flaps had scalloped edges. They didn't convey the professional touch she needed.

Running downstairs, she filched a couple of plain business envelopes from Daddy's desk.

To the Honorable Judge Mark Mayfield

Private and Confidential

URGENT

She printed in thick letters and underscored *Urgent* in red felt marker. She would take it to the judge herself. Mrs. Tobin said he still lived in the city but was expected back in Washington within days. The mail would take too long, and a hand delivery would get more attention.

Already a confident detective, she knew the first place to learn about Judge Mayfield was on the internet. His biography on Wikipedia was impressively long.

Judge Mark Quincy Mayfield.

Reading, she was encouraged by his rise through the judicial ranks. A man with his noble record would not refuse to assist two wrongly accused men. She had to get her letter into his hands and needed his home address.

She called the Municipal Court and, after a long wait on hold, was finally connected to the information desk.

"I'm calling from the Rockcastle Florist," she said, using Miss Bancroft to help her sound more mature. "We have an order for a magnificent floral arrangement for Judge Mark Mayfield. Would you please give us his home address so we can deliver it?"

"His home address?" a stern feminine voice questioned. "The judge isn't with this court, and we don't give out personal information."

"Perhaps in this case, you can make an exception. The floral arrangement is to congratulate him on his appointment to—"

She heard the dial tone and didn't know if she'd been deliberately cut off or accidentally disconnected. It didn't matter. She wasn't going to get Judge Mayfield's address from the court.

While on hold, she'd had time to plan her next move and placed another call. "The news room, please," she said when someone at the *Sun Times* answered.

The operator forwarded the call and, after a single ring, a man's voice said a snappy, "Travis."

Charlene decided this time a high school student might have better luck than Miss Bancroft. "I'm the editor of my high school newspaper."

Quickly, she explained that she hoped to do an interview Judge Mark Mayfield. "I'm not interested in the heavy stuff like they put on the news. I want to write an article about what he remembers from high school--like what he did for fun and what his favorite subjects were."

She heard a chuckle. "What's your name?"

"Charlene Rockcastle."

"Well, Charlene, it sounds like a great idea, but what can I do for you?"

"I want to deliver the letter personally. That's how I got an interview with the mayor, but I don't have his address."

"I think I can help you with that one. Hang on."

This time Charlene didn't mind waiting, and Travis wasn't gone long. "We have his home address. Do you have a pencil?"

He gave her the address. "I wish you luck, but Charlene, he's getting a lot of attention right now. I wouldn't bet on your chance of getting an interview."

"I would bet on it. Travis, you've been a great help."

Studying the address, she felt triumphant. Detective work suited her. She wanted to deliver the letter immediately and dressed for the occasion--proper shoes, not sandals, and a plain white blouse and dark skirt. She had never worn the skirt because it was too long, but now too long created the right effect. Standing in front of her mirrored closet door, she decided she might pass for an applicant to a convent.

According to her Mapquest search, the judge's address was twenty miles away and had to be near the lake. She could take the Outer Drive most of the way. Without stopping for breakfast, she left a note on the table saying she had an errand to run and ducked out of the house alone. As much as she loved her cousin, Dominique's failure to appreciate what she was doing was a downer.

Leaving the Outer Drive, she went through an area where Victorian style homes had been restored to what had to be close to their original splendor. She expected the judge's address to be one of the three-story houses with decorative facades, but it wasn't.

Following GPS directions, Charlene turned onto a broad street that paralleled the lake. To her surprise, she found that the judge's address was a contemporary stone high-rise surrounded by large, potted evergreen trees. A tunnel led to the building's underground parking lot. Charlene knew she had no chance of finding parking on the street and drove into the lot. At the guard house, she showed her driver's license to a uniformed officer.

"I have correspondence for Judge Markham," she said when he asked why she was there.

After studying her license, the officer pressed a lever to open the steel gate. Pointing, he directed her, and she pulled into the visitors' parking section. Getting out of the car, she opted for the escalator instead of the elevator and rode up into the building's spacious lobby.

She had expected to knock on the front door of a residence and hand the letter to anyone who answered. She hardly expected it to be the judge, but surely he had a housekeeper or someone else in attendance. No matter who came to the door, she was prepared to be very persuasive and insist that the letter was worthy of the judge's attention.

Not until she was in the building did she have doubts. Diffidence was not her thing, but the spacious and elegant foyer made her feel small. She was only eighteen, without a credential, trying to enlist the help of a man who would soon be sworn-in as a justice of the Supreme Court. No one would pay any attention to her. She took a deep breath. Perhaps it was foolish to have come, but she was here now.

"Miss, may I help you?" the doorman asked, approaching her. Standing a few feet behind him was a big, uniformed guard with a stern expression, a holstered gun, and a clipboard.

"I have an important letter for Judge Mayfield," she said, holding her head high in a show of confidence she didn't feel.

"What's your name?" the guard asked, checking the clipboard.

"Charlene Rockcastle, but you don't have my name. I came on my own. I'm trying to help two men charged with a murder they didn't commit." She talked rapidly, explaining she had proof they were innocent.

She saw the guard and doorman glance at each other and had the uneasy feeling they thought she was babbling. The guard said, "You can leave the letter in the mailroom."

Charlene shook her head. "This is desperately important." Her voice pitched higher than she intended. "Please, is there any way I can personally hand it to someone to take to the judge?"

The guard said, "The judge's housekeeper usually arrives about now. If you leave your letter with me, I might be able to get her to take it. If I can't, it goes to the mailroom."

The guard and doorman looked at her as if she were a silly juvenile. Talk about giving it to the housekeeper was meant to get her out of there quietly. As soon as she left, her letter would go to the mailroom, but she wasn't going to do any better. After she handed the letter it to the guard, she couldn't get away fast enough and ran down a moving escalator.

CHAPTER 38

The guard hadn't taken her seriously. Worse, he and the doorman had acted amused. Failure was a rare experience for Charlene and, driving out of the underground parking lot, she felt ridiculous, exhausted, and very hungry.

A nap would have to wait until she was home, but she had skipped breakfast and deserved something to eat now. Fast food would work, but she remembered passing a chain restaurant she knew and liked. She had no trouble finding it and parked in the lot behind the building.

Inside, a waiter led her to a small table by a window. When he handed her a menu, she started to giggle. She couldn't stop and, alone with nothing in front of her but a menu, she giggled until she had to catch her breath.

"Is anything wrong, Miss?"

"Nothing's wrong," she gasped. "I'll have bacon and waffles with powdered sugar."

She stared out the window, not wanting to see the reaction of other patrons to her giggling fit. They couldn't know that she had been making fun of herself. She had run with the crazy idea that, on her own, she could solve a murder.

Dominique had been right to discourage her. What she was planning wasn't just nonsense. It was irresponsible, starting with reading Nick Crane's letter and tricking Mr. Jerry Finlay into giving her information. Linking her two sources together, she had forged a theory: *Bart Corbin had been killed by a man he had protected in a murder investigation, and the man's initials were MOM.*

It could actually be true, but it had been brainless of her to think that, acting alone, she could get Judge Mayfield to help her prove it. Good grief, soon he would be confirmed as *Justice* Mayfield. She had succeeded with the mayor, but this time she had stepped too far outside the lines. Worse, her motive had been to launch a career as a detective. Saving two innocent men hadn't been nearly as important as her career. The situation didn't seem funny anymore. She was selfish and felt a wave of guilt.

The waiter set her order in front of her, then paused. "Miss, is there anything else I can do?" he asked gently.

She was ready to take a bite of waffle and shook her head. He was probably concerned because of her giggling fit, but that mood was broken. Thinking about how selfish her motives had been, she could feel tears welling up. She blinked hard. If she went from giggles to tears over a waffle, onlookers would be on the lookout for her keeper.

She decided that as soon as she saw Daddy, she would tell him everything she knew — or thought she knew — about the Barton Corbin murder case. He would know what to do, and that would be the end of it for her. Of course, he would voice his disapproval of her efforts. That was the downside of having an attorney for a father. They could be very long and detailed in stating their case.

Her emotional hodge-podge didn't keep her from enjoying her food. She felt better. Perhaps, all she had needed was something to eat.

When she got home, Dominique told her that her father was taking a deposition and would be late. "Your mother went to visit her sister. She said tonight we could order in Chinese for dinner."

Charlene wasn't interested in Chinese. It had been a long drive home through sluggish traffic. She needed to rest and yawning, headed to her bedroom.

The blinds were open, but the bedroom was already dark when the phone rang. Charlene had been asleep for hours. Reaching for the receiver, she knocked over a glass of water. She picked up the receiver and managed a groggy hello.

A deep, masculine voice said, "I'm Judge Mark Mayfield's clerk. He received a letter that interested him. It gave this phone number."

Charlene tried to blink herself awake. Was she still dreaming or was this actually happening?

"The judge asked me to find out who wrote the letter. Is that person available?"

"I wrote it," Charlene said, opening her eyes wide to come awake.

"What is your name?"

When she told him, he responded with a quick barrage of questions. "Where did you get your information?"

She explained about Mr. Finlay. "He's not on the case anymore, but he thought Bart Corbin might have been an alibi in an unsolved murder."

Awake and excited, she told him everything she knew. "A witness is certain he saw the murderer in the park."

He said the words one at a time. "What is the witness's name?"

"Nick Crane."

"Nick Crane," he repeated. After a brief silence, he said a soft, "You know what you're talking about."

It was her case again. She wanted to help solve it, but now her concern was for the imprisoned men, not her success. That Judge Mayfield was taking an interest was a miracle. God was pleased with her change of attitude and was on the team.

The judge's helper asked her to explain again how she managed to get the information. She tried not to sound proud when she said, "I handled the investigation myself. I'm going to be a detective." She made a correction. "I *am* a detective."

"A good one," he said. "A very good one if you've kept what you know secret."

Charlene assured him she hadn't told anyone. "It's my case. No one has any idea I'm working on it." It was true. Dominique could have been in on it but didn't want to be.

"Excellent work," he said. "I will explain everything to Judge Mayfield and call you back in about an hour. Promise you won't talk about this to anyone. Under the circumstances, it might be very dangerous."

Promising, she started to call him by name, then realized she didn't know it. "Sir, you'll call me back in an hour?" she asked.

"I think so." The line went dead.

Charlene looked for Dominique. She couldn't tell her about the phone call but gave her a big hug.

"You seem different than when you came home. What happened?"

"Nothing happened, nothing at all."

Dominique looked skeptical, but Charlene didn't care. Someday, she could tell her cousin the whole story.

It was the longest hour in the history of the world. The clock crawled until it had been an hour and a half, then two hours. Charlene was beginning to wonder if she had dreamt the call, but the tipped over water glass told her it had really happened. She hated the smell of cigarette smoke, but almost wished she had the habit and could puff away with Dominique on the back patio.

The phone rang. "I'll get it," Charlene screeched, shooing Dominique away. "Hello."

It was the same voice. "Judge Mayfield wants to meet with you personally. It has to be very private. If the media learned about a meeting, your name would get out. It might be danger-ous for you. He doesn't want to put you in harm's way."

"Tomorrow morning, I can go to his office and--"

He cut her off. "The judge is leaving. It has to be tonight. Are you familiar with North Avenue Beach?"

When she told him she wasn't, he gave her directions. "There's a boathouse. It's deserted this time of year, and the judge will meet you there. Be there in two hours. Don't look for the judge. He'll find you."

When he asked for her description, she said she was a tall bru-nette but hesitated when he wanted her age. She took a breath. "Twenty-eight." It wasn't a lie. She would be twenty-eight in less than a decade.

His final words were a kindly, "Dress warm."

Charlene was ecstatic. This was her first clandestine meeting as a detective and with a truly eminent person. Her pounding heart told her she had found her calling.

When Dominique realized Charlene was going out, she decided to be a nuisance. "I'm going with you," she insisted.

"I don't want you to," Charlene said. "I'm meeting a friend."

Usually passive, Dominique was suddenly adamant. "I don't know what you're planning, but I don't like it. Charlene, I mean it. You're not leaving without me."

Charlene finally gave in. "You have to promise not to ask questions or tell anyone."

"I promise," Dominique said. "Let me get my coat. She ran upstairs.

After several minutes, Charlene got impatient. It shouldn't take so long to pick up a coat. "Are you coming?" she called.

"Sorry," Dominique said, returning. "There was something I had to do."

CHAPTER 39

As soon as Mass was over, Philip phoned his daughter. It was still a thrill when he heard her say, "Hi, Dad."

When he asked what plans she and Charlene had for the day, she told him Charlene had gone out. "She left a note saying she had an errand to run. I don't know when she'll be back, but I'm fine. This is such a lovely place, and everyone is so good to me."

He had just ended his call with Dominique when the phone rang. Answering, he recognized the slightly arrogant lilt and knew what was coming. "Father, the bishop wants to see you this afternoon. May I tell him you'll be here?"

It sounded like a question, but Philip knew it was a summons. He wasn't in the mood to give the right answer. "Please, tell the bishop I am sorry, but I can't make it. If it is convenient for him, I can be there early tomorrow."

Putting off his bishop was unusual, especially when he didn't give a reason, but he wasn't ready to deal with the bishop's reaction to his television appearance. Their time in New York had brought him closer to his daughter, but realizing what she had endured sickened him. In addition to the limitations put on her by an invalid mother, the man she thought was her father had abused her. Her real father desperately wanted to help her in every way he could, but first he had to deal with his anger and confusion. He was hardly in the mood to be chastised.

According to Marge and Charles, Dominique was a very welcome guest. The words hadn't actually been spoken, but Philip knew she could continue to stay with them. Even if he wasn't providing for her, she was with family. Much as he wanted to contribute, he knew his brother would refuse any financial help.

It was obvious Charlene cared about her cousin, almost looking after her. That delighted Philip, but Charles had told him he was concerned about their girls. "Charlene has too much time on her hands," he had said. "She's acting mysterious. Whatever she's up to, I'm sure she's involved Dominique."

Philip couldn't tell his brother that Charlene was playing detective. Dominique had told him in confidence, and he couldn't give her away. He wasn't worried. With Charlene leading, they might drum up some mischief, but couldn't put themselves in any danger.

The bishop's office phoned again. "Bishop Corday is leaving for a conference tomorrow and is very anxious to see you. May I tell him you'll be here at four o'clock?"

The second call had the effect, not of a summons, but of a command. Philip said he would be there. If he'd any doubts about why he was sent for him, they vanished the moment he stepped through the massive doors to the bishop's office.

After the briefest of greetings, the bishop pointed him to a chair. "Father Rockcastle, you and your daughter appeared on television. It was a serious breach of obedience, and I must take that into account. However," His voice slowed, "when I instructed you not to talk about her, I had just been made aware of the situation. On reflection, I no longer think my admonition was necessarily in the best interest of the church."

His hands, for once motionless, rested on his desk. "Indeed, your experience reflects the hand of God. People should find it very inspirational. I'm sure you realize you were wrong to disobey me, but you now have my permission to talk about your daughter."

Since he had already shared his story with a large television audience, permission was being given after the fact. Philip had the feeling that, hidden somewhere in the bishop's words, was a hint of apology.

"My housekeeper taped the program, and I had the opportunity to see it. I was impressed with the way the audience rejoiced for you. There were no negative suspicions. They applauded long and with enthusiasm when you said your reunion with your daughter was the hand of God." He smiled, "She seems like a lovely young lady. Has she been baptized?"

"I baptized her on the day she was born."

"The day she was born?" Bishop Corday repeated. "Did the doctors think she might die?"

Philip envisioned her in his arms. "She was perfectly healthy--a beautiful, seven-pound baby girl."

Leaning toward him, the bishop asked, "Why did you baptize her?"

Philip shrugged. "Suddenly, I was just doing it. When I thought she was dead, the memory comforted me. I thought I had been divinely inspired, because she wouldn't live until her formal baptism." His chest heaved. "I was wrong."

"Philip, you weren't wrong," the bishop said, using his name for the first time. "Of course, the memory comforted you. It was divine inspiration to make your pain bearable when you thought your child was dead."

Since being reunited with his daughter, Philip had thought about that spontaneous baptism many times and was no longer convinced providence had guided him. It was just something he had done in an exuberant moment, but the bishop was right. The memory of the hospital room baptism had made the pain more endurable. Of course, he had been guided. He wanted to believe it.

He realized the bishop was talking. "You said she attended your catechism class. Are you instructing her in the faith?"

Philip had never thought about it. Maybe, somewhere down the road when they were used to each other, he could bring up Catholicism. At the moment, he was satisfied with her just the way she was. If she decided to join the church, it would be wonderful. It was too late for him to step into the role of supervising parent.

When the bishop opened a desk drawer, Philip thought he was being dismissed. Instead, the bishop took out a small, white jewelry box and held it out to him. "This is for Dominique. It is from the diocese...and from me."

Opening it, Philip saw a beautiful, gold cross on a delicate chain.

"Tell her it comes with our blessings and prayers."

Thanking him, Philip stood up. Bishop Corday held out his hand and Philip kissed his ring.

There was more than one way to interpret divine guidance. Walking out through the carved, oak doors, Philip sensed a cloud was beginning to lift.

CHAPTER 40

"Philip, do you know where our girls are? We haven't heard from Charlene, and her cell phone is turned off."

It was late, and the girls were unaccounted for. It wasn't news Philip wanted to hear. He told his brother, "Dominique said Charlene was playing detective. I didn't mention it, because she told me in confidence. You had better listen to this." Holding the phone to the answering machine, he played Dominique's message.

"Dad, Charlene is going out. She's acting very excited. I think she's planning to catch a murderer. She doesn't want me along, but I won't let her go alone." Charlene's voice was heard shouting, "Cousin, I'm leaving." The message broke off with a quick good-bye.

"So that's it," Charles said. "My investigator phoned this afternoon. He's concerned because someone with access to my office impersonated Persy Bancroft trying to get information about the Corbin case. Persy thinks the impersonator had to be Charlene."

"Did you ask Charlene about it?"

"I haven't had a chance, but what Dominique told you gives me the answer. According to Jerry Finlay, the impersonator thinks the indicted men are innocent. It's Charlene. Good grief, I hope she doesn't have the crazy idea she can catch the actual murderer."

Philip vaguely remembered that when he returned from New York, Nick Crane's letter was lying unfolded atop his desk. "Charles, I have a letter Charlene may have read."

With so much on his mind, he had hardly paid attention. Now he ferreted the letter from the pile, and read it to his brother. "The man's name is crossed out. I don't think she could have deciphered it."

"She likes programs on forensics and might know a way. Phil, you have to get a hold of the man who wrote that letter and find out who he saw. The girls might try something and get in over their heads."

Philip didn't need to be coaxed. As soon as he hung up, he checked the church directory. The address for Mrs. Marie Crane was on Oakleigh Street. He didn't phone. He could better evaluate what Nick told him if they were face to face.

Mrs. Crane answered the bell. "Father Rockcastle," she said, as casually as if he showed up at her door every day, "Please, come in."

"I know it's late, but I need to talk to Nick."

She offered Philip a seat in the living room and went to get her husband. He appeared carrying a paperback novel.

"You're here because of my letter," he said to Philip. No preamble, no hello.

"Nick, I think my niece may have managed to read the name you crossed out. My daughter is with her, and I'm afraid they might try something reckless. I need to know who it was."

Nick didn't hesitate. "I saw the Honorable Mark Q. Mayfield in Humboldt Park, right after he murdered Barton Corbin."

His wife gasped. "Nick, you don't know what you're saying. Mark Mayfield is going to be confirmed as a Supreme Court justice." She turned to Philip. "Father, I knew he'd go crazy if he kept reading all that crime garbage. I wouldn't be surprised if he has a picture of Ann Rule in his wallet."

Ignoring her, Nick said, "I knew Mayfield for years and I recognized him. Better than that, he knew me and called me Snowball."

"Nick, listen to me. That's crazy." Marie Crane was a small woman with a genteel demeanor, but was obviously used to holding her own.

Philip had to wait while they bickered. It gave him time to think. Nick's claim that he and Judge Mayfield recognized each other was certainly possible, but the idea that the honored judge had committed a murder was insane.

"Nick, I want you to tell me--" His phone rang. "It's my brother," he said. "I have to take this."

"Philip, I went through Charlene's wastebasket. She discarded several letters addressed to Judge Mark Mayfield. She said she had information that could free two men charged with murder. It gets garbled, and she mentions a letter and initials on a class ring."

When his brother said "Mark Mayfield," Philip repeated the name. When the Cranes heard it, the bickering was over. Hanging up, he had their attention, but what his brother told him didn't make sense. If Charlene actually thought Mayfield was a murderer, why would she write to him?

When Philip wondered aloud, Nick said, "He's been getting plenty of attention. She might have thought he was a dedicated judge who might help her. If she wrote and told him what she knew--"

"She would be a threat to him," Philip said, finishing the thought. It was impossible, insane, but *if* Mayfield had killed to hide an earlier crime, he might kill again. A conviction for three murders wouldn't be worse than a conviction for two—*or four.*

"We have to notify the police." Standing up, he started to dial 911.

Nick leapt up and pushed Philip's hand off his phone. "The police won't issue an arrest warrant for Mark Mayfield. They'll think you're nuts. We have to figure all the angles and decide what to do."

Philip stared at him, blank. Without the police, all they could do was wait.

"Q lured Corbin to Humboldt Park," Nick said. "It was a place he knew. If he tries anything with the girls, he'll need a familiar place again. It can't be the park. He wouldn't plan anything there a second time."

Marie started to say something, but Nick shook his head, hushing her. He didn't want to be interrupted. "There was an article about him in the Sunday Supplement. In one picture, he was on his yacht. I think it was named the *Legality*." There was a pause, then Nick repeated, "The *Legality*."

"Marie! Where is the equipment I saved from the Coast Guard?"

"That old stuff? It's in a wooden chest in the back of the garage."

"Come on, Rockcastle," Nick said. "We'll take my truck."

Philip wavered, not knowing what Nick had in mind, but his daughter and niece might be in danger. Doing anything had to be better than doing nothing.

The truck was in the driveway and, going outside, he waited while Nick lugged gear from the garage and loaded it in the back.

"When you do detective work," Nick said, "you should be prepared."

Nick's urgency was convincing, but not until they were driving did Philip ask where they were going. Nick said, "I have a strong hunch--" Interrupting himself, he said, "Did you see how that stupid galoot made a turn?"

Nick soon identified a couple more galoots. Philip didn't know what a galoot was, but suspected Nick ran into them every time he drove. He appreciated the distraction. It gave him time to realize he was being irrational.

Charlene might try to play detective, but what could she actually do? A letter she wrote yesterday could not have reached Judge Mayfield. More important, the judge had been investigated and interrogated by the United States Senate. The slightest shade in his past would have been discovered and examined under bright lights.

Nick stopped taking note of galoots long enough to ask, "What color car are they driving?"

"My niece's car is blue, a Camaro I think. Let's go back and wait to hear from the girls."

Nick had to have heard but didn't respond. Instead, he kept barreling down the street. Talk about galoots.

Nick drove onto a beach parking lot. It was after hours and empty. Circling back on to the road, he checked a couple of other parking areas. Philip knew it was a waste, but didn't say anything. Nick was hell-bent and wasn't going to listen.

When it started to drizzle, Nick returned to the main road. Philip thought he was heading home. Instead, he made a sharp turn and started down a narrow path. The headlights caught the outline of a black car parked on the narrow shoulder. They drove closer. The black car turned blue.

CHAPTER 41

There's a guardrail at the end of the street. To the left of it is a narrow road. Watch for it. It may be hard to see.

Remembering her instructions, Charlene turned onto a strip of pavement that was more path than road. It bordered the sand on one side. A tangle of trees and bushes on the other side loomed as dark shadows in the headlights.

Dominique braced her hand against the dashboard and looked around. "What are we doing here?"

"This is where I was told to park."

"That's weird. Who told you?"

Without answering, Charlene got out of the car. Dominique followed, muttering, "I don't like this."

Charlene was about to remind Dominique she had agreed not to ask questions, but changed her mind. Like it or not, her cousin was here. "You can never tell anyone — at least not yet — but I'm going to meet Judge Mark Mayfield."

"You're here to meet a judge? That doesn't make sense." Glancing around, Dominique complained that it was dark. The beach looks deserted."

"That's the idea," Charlene said, her excitement growing. "I'm supposed to walk in this direction." Pointing, she started out across the sand. When Dominique didn't follow, she said, "You insisted on coming, and I can't leave you here alone. Hurry up."

With Dominique trudging behind her, Charlene continued walking, her shoes filling with sand. She pointed into the darkness. "I think I see the concession stand."

Judge Mayfield's clerk had told Charlene the judge would meet her at a concession stand that was deserted this time of year. Reaching it, she thought it looked deserted, period. The long, one-story building had a roof with a low over-hang. A timber with a scalloped edge dangled. It probably had once been trim. The window frames were empty. The wooden walk across the front was broken and uneven. A clutter of bricks lay near the wide doorway.

There was no light; no one called out to her. Looking around, she saw Dominique pick something up. She started to ask her cousin what she had found when she heard a whispered, "Miss Rockcastle."

She spun toward the sound. "Where are you?"

"I'm here." A shadow moved out of the darkness. A thread of light beamed from a small flashlight. She had expected Judge Mayfield, but the voice was the voice she had heard on the phone.

"Where's the judge?" she asked.

"He's waiting, but you have someone with you."

"Dominique is my cousin. She understands that this meeting has to be kept secret. You can trust her," Charlene said.

"Two of you," he said. "Are you sure no one else knows you're here? You followed my instructions and didn't tell anyone?"

"I haven't talked to anyone but Dominique since I talked to you."

Dominique cried, "Charlene, you did. You told someone."

"Silly, I did not." Squinting, Charlene couldn't see past the flashlight beam to make out his face and spoke to the blackness. "Sir, she's wrong."

"That's good...but there are two of you," he said again.

Dominique said, "This is creepy. I want to go back to the car."

Her cousin was wrong. It wasn't creepy. It was exciting, and there was nothing to be afraid of. A meeting with Judge Mayfield was such a miracle, God must have arranged it. They were perfectly safe, and she wouldn't miss it for the world.

"We shouldn't keep the judge waiting," the voice said, starting to walk toward the lapping sound of the water.

Dominique grabbed Charlene's arm. "Let's not go."

"You insisted on coming. Now, you're acting like a baby. Come with us or go back to the car."

He turned around, fixing the flashlight beam on them. "Miss Rockcastle, we can't leave her here alone." Addressing Dominique, he said, "Come with us, my dear. It won't take long."

Dominique still held Charlene's arm as they followed him across the sand, his tiny flashlight marking a pale path. When he shone the flashlight ahead, Charlene saw they were approaching a long pier.

"Hurry," he said. "The judge is waiting."

"Why doesn't he come here?" Dominique asked.

"You'll see."

They reached the pier. Walking was easier on the wooden planks. Charlene was surprised to see a yacht tied up at the far end, and Dominique's grip on her arm became a vise.

Reaching the yacht, the man tugged the line to pull it closer. "The water's too shallow here to use the ladder. We have to step from the pier onto the deck."

Dominique clung to her. "Charlene, this can't be right. Let's go back."

"No! I didn't want you to come, and I won't let you spoil this." The whole scene was thrilling. Her first case would be a high benchmark for other cases to follow. It might be a little spooky, but a good detective had to know when to take risks.

Charlene wanted Dominique to go first, afraid that if she went first her cousin might head back to the car. Dominique refused. She would follow but definitely would not lead.

The yacht appeared totally dark, and it made a lonely sound as it rose and fell to the rhythm of the waves. The water looked black and ominous. Despite herself, Charlene felt a dawning panic. Returning to the car might not be a bad idea. Quick, she had to make a decision; stay and meet the judge or let Dominique think she was a coward and live with regrets.

Taking a deep breath, she stretched from the pier, grasped the side of the yacht, and climbed aboard. Dominique followed quickly. She dropped something on the deck and bent to look for it, but the yacht rocked hard and she staggered.

He climbed aboard after them. "Did you hear that splash?" he asked. "It was my cell phone. It slipped out of my pocket." He peered over the side. "No chance of fishing it out. It would be ruined anyway. Let me use yours so I can let him know we're here."

Charlene pulled her phone out of her purse and handed it to him. After a moment, he said, "It's not working. The battery may be low." He reached a hand toward Dominique. "Let me try yours."

Dominique said. "I'll keep mine."

"Uncle Philip said he was going to get you a phone. I didn't know you had it already."

"Charlene!"

He opened the door to the cabin and beamed the light inside. "Wait in there. When I get the generator going, the light will come on."

Dominique clutched Charlene's arm again. "You told Charlene the judge was waiting. There's no one here."

"You're wrong, my dear. The judge is on board. He wants you to wait in the cabin."

When they entered the cabin, the door closed behind them. Trying to open it, Dominique cried out, "Please, open the door. It's stuck." Charlene helped her tug the handle, but the door didn't budge.

"What's that noise?" Dominique asked, her voice rising.

"It must be the generator," Charlene said. Before the words were out, she knew better. It sounded like a motor trying to turn over.

She knelt on the cold floor. What was happening was baffling, but she wasn't worried. Judge Mayfield was responsible for their situation, and the President had appointed him to one of highest positions in the country. He had been confirmed by the Senate. Since she first learned his name, she had heard it mentioned many times.

Mentioned many times.

What had Nick Crane said?

Corbin must have figured with his name plastered in the news, it was time to tighten the screws.

Suddenly, Charlene had a strange, hollow feeling. The idea was insane. It wasn't possible. It wasn't. But her letter had been marked personal and private. Only the judge was supposed to read it, but the man who brought them here had read it. She had hardly glimpsed his face and couldn't tell if he looked like the picture in the internet article about Judge Mark Quincy Mayfield.

She murmured the name aloud. *Mark Quincy Mayfield.*

Nick Crane's letter said the man he saw was nicknamed by his middle initial. The initials on the ring Bart Corbin had were

M.O.M. Fighting dizziness not caused by the motion of the yacht, Charlene envisioned an engraved Q. The tail grew faint. It became an O.

She was so smart, so clever, such a good detective, yet she had failed to see what was right in front of her. Never had she tried to match the pieces —-Yale, the neighborhood, everything--but how could she suspect an honored judge?

Dominique sat down on the floor close to her. "Charlene," she whispered. "I don't think the judge is coming."

Charlene's throat felt tight. "The judge is here."

Her letter made her a threat. She shuddered but not from the cold. He intended to take them far out on the lake and leave them there. She could almost feel the weight being tied around her. Mom and Daddy would never know what happened to her. They would search forever, half in grief, half in hope. Uncle Philip, Poor Uncle Philip. He had just been reunited with his daughter. He would pray for another miraculous reunion, but it would never happen. And Dominique? Her cousin had tried to protect her and had been smart enough to be afraid. Now a weight would be found for her.

"Dominique...oh Cousin," she gasped, "He wants to kill us. We have to do something."

"I was afraid every minute, but I couldn't leave you." She struck a match.

"There's no time to smoke." Charlene said, then realized her cousin wasn't lighting a cigarette. She was holding the match high and searching the cabin.

Charlene heard the sound again, a motor trying to turn over. This time it did. They were starting to move.

Dominique struck another match and circled it around the cabin. A cushioned bench was against the wall. There were a couple of deck chairs, and a small, cast-iron table. It looked heavy, the top a set-in piece of glass.

"Dominique, hold a match by the table." Studying it, she said, "If we broke the glass, we could use big pieces to defend ourselves." She grabbed an afghan off the bench and spread it on the floor.

The match went out. Dominique lit another.

Struggling, Charlene turned the table upside down on the afghan and lifted the heavy base away from the glass. Bringing the base down hard, she shattered the glass.

Peering over the pieces with a match, they each picked up a shard. Jerking the rod from the little window, Charlene pulled off the curtains. The material was flimsy, but they used it to wrap the shards, trying to leave a sharp edge exposed.

"I wish I had my brick," Dominique said.

"What are you talking about?"

"I looked for something to use as a club. I found a brick but dropped it when I climbed on board."

Charlene was too preoccupied to think about bricks. "Let's each hold a leg of the table and swing it hard against the door. If we get out, we can protect ourselves with the glass."

Dominique couldn't help while holding a match, so in darkness they swung the table hard against the door. It took three swings to make a hole large enough for Charlene to reach through to the latch. The judge had to have heard the banging. Hopefully, he would think they were still pounding from inside the cabin. As she opened the door, the yacht bounced hard. She almost lost her balance.

The light drizzle she'd felt walking across the sand was becoming a steady rain. Each holding a piece of glass, they crawled onto the slippery deck. They couldn't stand; the bouncing and the rain kept them on their knees. Dominique started crawling around. Charlene wanted her to say close, but was afraid to call her.

Charlene could see the judge's dark outline at the wheel. Suddenly, Dominique was standing behind him, her hands raised high. She was hitting him with something and screaming for Charlene. Yelling and cursing, Judge Mayfield was trying to fight her off but couldn't get to his feet.

Charlene scrambled to help. The glass shard was useless. She couldn't stab him through his jacket. Dominique was still hitting him. His arms waved wildly as he reached for her, but she was behind him and he couldn't get turned around. Charlene threw herself at him, her weight holding him in place for Dominique's blows. When he went limp, Dominique hit him one more time. She had found her brick.

They were both drenched from the rain and crying. The yacht was bouncing out of control. Lights dotting the shoreline were getting dimmer.

"We're going straight out into the lake," Charlene sobbed. "I have to steer."

On their knees, they tugged Judge Mayfield's motion-less body away from the controls. Charlene got behind the wheel. She had never driven a boat, but a throttle shouldn't be difficult to operate. Forward had to accelerate. In moments, they were going faster but in the wrong direction. As Charlene maneuvered into a turn, the yacht started to tip. Water flooded over the side.

Dominique screamed, "We're going to capsize."

Charlene jerked the wheel back. This wasn't a car. She couldn't make a sharp turn. She waited until the yacht stopped bouncing, and she had hold of herself before she tried again, this time turning in a wide arc.

Dominique shouted, "He probably headed straight out from the pier to keep anyone on shore from seeing him."

It made sense, not that it mattered. Charlene didn't care where they came ashore as long as they did. She steered in as straight a direction as she could, but holding a boat steady on a turbulent lake was a different experience than cruising the Outer Drive.

There were lights ahead. They were almost to shore.

"Get away from the wheel."

Judge Mayfield was conscious and holding a gun. Charlene and Dominique reached for each other and hugged tight.

CHAPTER 42

Philip bolted from the truck while Nick was still braking. Hoping it wasn't, he knew it was, and Charlene's car would only be here if she had come to meet someone. She had not come alone. His Dominique was with her.

"We don't know how much head start they have," Nick said, taking items from the back of the truck. "Here, you carry this." He thrust a long-handled flashlight at Philip, then picked up what looked like a big horn. Heading toward the lake, he ran down the pavement and onto the sand.

` Nick obviously knew where he was going. Philip kept close pace behind him although fear made his legs want to buckle.

The rain was picking up. It was coming down harder by the time they reached a long pier. Running the length of the pier, Nick shouted for Philip to bring him the flashlight. Almost snatching it from Philip's hand, he turned it on and shone it onto the water, circling the beam in all directions. Rain caught the light and created a blinding cascade of falling crystals.

Philip stared out, unsure of what he was looking for. Nick had said Mayfield had a yacht. If that is what they expected to find--if Mayfield had the girls out on the lake—all they could do was pray.

All they could do was pray and wait for the bodies to wash ashore.

Sinking to his knees, Philip did pray, but not to God. "Susanna, forgive me for not realizing the baby in your arms was not our baby. Our little girl was abused. It was my fault. I should have known--I should have..."

Lightening, brilliant and all-consuming, struck close above him. Its fierce power blanked all thought. Still on his knees, Philip floated in a stunned abyss. The light faded. The only sound was the pounding rain. Thunder roared. The force of it stunned him. As the sound faded, he felt different. Despite the rain, despite everything, a new reality was dawning.

Standing up, he shouted into the rain. "No! It *wasn't* my fault. I didn't know."

Of course, he hadn't known. For the first time, he acknowledged that the bus had not turned over because God willed it. It had just happened. "It was an accident." He said it aloud. "An accident."

Nick was tugging his arm. "Look!"

There was a light, faint, out on the water. It was getting brighter and approaching the pier. "That's her," Nick shouted.

"It's Mayfield's yacht. She's coming this way." Beaming the flashlight toward the yacht, he muttered, "Damn it. Damn it."

The yacht start to circle until it was headed toward deep water. Nick raised his horn. The loudest human voice Philip had ever heard boomed, "Attention *Legality*, you are under surveillance by the United States Coast Guard. Mayfield, you have two passengers on board. Bring them to dock here, immediately. Repeat, *Legality*, this is the United States Coast Guard. You are under surveillance. Bring your passengers to dock."

The yacht tossed high in the stormy water. Tipping to starboard, she was ready to capsize. Agonizing seconds passed as they watched in helpless silence. The *Legality* righted, turned slowly, not unto the lake but toward the pier.

Philip knew they were too late. Mayfield had been headed in. He had finished what he had to do and must have wanted to tie up until the rain subsided enough for him to return to his usual moorings. When he saw their light, he had changed his mind and headed back out until Nick ordered him in.

Philip could no longer feel the rain. He couldn't feel anything. His daughter and his brother's daughter were out there in the watery blackness.

Nick was calling the police. "Judge Mark Mayfield is on his yacht near the North Avenue Pier," he shouted. "He's in trouble. Alert the Coast Guard and send police backup."

Philip realized Nick said Mayfield was in trouble to get quick action. He hadn't said the honored judge had done anything wrong and risk sounding like a nutcase to be ignored.

All they could do was wait. Philip was oblivious to time. Was it only a few minutes or did it take awhile before headlights beamed across the sand toward them?

Two patrol cars pulled up. Nick was ready with explanations. The officers were probably dubious but, as soon as the yacht was close enough to the pier, two of them grasped her side and pulled themselves aboard. "The judge is here," one of them shouted. "He's okay, and two females are tied up in fish nets."

They weren't out in the water. They were alive! Bursting, Philip put his leg over the side and pulled himself onto the deck.

"Dad!" He heard Dominique's piercing cry, and then saw her and Charlene lying on the deck bound with ropes and a tangle of in fish netting.

"You're okay now. You're okay," he repeated, helping the officer struggling to cut them loose. When they were free, he held Charlene's hand to help her onto the pier, then he helped Dominique. He followed and pulled them both into his arms. They were crying.

"Uncle Philip, I was right," Charlene gasped between sobs. "He told us he did it." Slumping against him, she fainted. Two officers took over and carried her toward a patrol car.

Philip kissed Dominique's face, wet with hot tears and cold rain. Holding her, he didn't know the words to tell her what she meant to him.

With more police crowding the scene, Philip didn't actually see Mayfield, but he heard Nick call out, "Q, I beat you to the pier this time."

On the way to the police station, Philip sat in the back seat with the girls. He kept an arm around each of them, holding tight. Nick followed in his truck. They were all taken to the captain's office and given blankets and hot coffee. A stenographer took Charlene's statement. Her fainting attack was over. She was in command.

"He locked us in the cabin. We fought our way out, and Dominique pounded him over the head with our brick."

"It was my brick. I found it on the shore," Dominique's voice was soft but proud.

"We thought she killed him. I took charge of the yacht and headed back to shore. Steering was difficult but I managed."

Charlene continued, her usual confidence returning. "We didn't know he was still alive until he came at us with a gun. He said he'd had to kill Bart and was sorry he had to kill us."

Dominique interrupted. "I yelled at him. I told him if he shot us, our blood would be all over his boat. He couldn't get away with it. He'd be caught."

Charlene added, "No one was steering. We were bouncing and couldn't stand up. That's when he dropped the net over us."

Dominique was sitting next to Philip and leaned close. "Dad, I didn't see the net until I was all tangled up. I was sure he was going to take us out on the lake and force us overboard. He would have, too, but we heard the United States Coast Guard. The Coast Guard saved us."

"It wasn't the Coast Guard. Nick, you saved them," Philip said.

There weren't enough chairs in the office, and Nick stood with his back to the wall. When the captain questioned him, he acted surprisingly diffident for a man with notable bluster.

"How did you know Judge Mayfield would lure the girls on to his yacht?"

"Mayfield returned to familiar territory to take care of Corbin. I figured all the angles and decided that's what he would try."

The lieutenant said, "You would be a great detective."

Nick said a quiet, "Everything I know, I learned from Sherlock."

Dominique said, "I don't get it. Does this mean you alerted the Coast Guard to protect us?"

Nick cupped his hands around his mouth. "*Legality*, this is the United States Coast Guard. Return to dock. Jane Doe, I said it louder when I had my bullhorn."

"It was you! she repeated, standing up. "But I'm not Jane Doe. I'm Dominique Rockcastle."

He laughed. "You can call me Snowball."

Philip didn't know who made the first move, but the former Jane Doe and Snowball hugged each other.

In the commotion, someone had contacted Charles and Marge. They arrived panicked until they saw for themselves that their daughter and niece were wet and weary, but safe.

"Daddy, I should have listened to Dominique," Charlene said, her voice uncharacteristically demure. "She didn't want us to go, and she knew right away that something was wrong."

Charles embraced his own daughter and then Dominique, saying, "Your mother would be proud of you."

The brothers acknowledged each other in a wordless exchange. Long explanations would come later. The girls had made their statements and were eager to leave.

"My car," Charlene exclaimed. "We have to go back to the beach so I can get it."

"We can get the car tomorrow," Dominique said. "Now we're going back to your house." Her tone had the impact of a stamping foot.

Philip grinned. The determined girl who had stood on his doorstep still existed and had shown better judgment than her straight-A student cousin.

He helped Charles and Marge usher the girls to their car. They would be well taken care of, and he would see them in the morning.

On the drive to Nick's house, there were no more galoots, no conversation, until they pulled up by Philip's car.

"I won't be at your class again."

"I know."

"I might go to Mass once with Marie. I'll sit in the front pew so you can see me."

"I'd like that. Marie would, too, but it will have to be soon."

Philip had almost lost his daughter a second time. This man had saved her. He had to thank him in a way that would mean something. Heading to his car, he called, "The next time you start an argument, I'll let you win."

"I'll win on my own." Nick's front door slammed.
Philip was still able to laugh.

CHAPTER 43

Despite the hour, there was something he had to do, some-one he had to see. It couldn't wait until morning. He didn't have the address, but remembered the house. Senora Garcia wouldn't open it until he convinced her he was Father Rockcastle.

"Dios mio! What is so wrong?"

"Nothing's wrong. I have good news. The man who mur-dered Barton Corbin is in police custody."

There was no need to identify the man. By noon, the media would be saturated with the details. "My brother will arrange for Rico and Leonard to be released on bond until charges against them are formally dropped."

Her black hair hung on her nightdress in two long braids. She looked strangely like a little girl. Crying, she grabbed his hand. "I knew you would help us. You are a man of God."

He *was* a man of God. All men were of God.

First light was threading in the east before Philip pulled into his driveway. Before getting out of the car, he studied the hazy silhouette of his church. The old brick structure had been the place of worship for a procession of ethnicities--German in the long ago, then strongly Polish, now Hispanic. Someday, people who praised God in yet another language would come to fill the pews. Other priests would take hi place at the altar. There would be another pastor. He would not be the last, but this was his last church, his last little while as a priest.

He had been called to the church and had served with gratitude and honor, but that was the past. All there was or ever could be was now, and now he was called to a life with Tara and their children, Dominique, Derek, and David. It had all worked out, exactly as God planned.

CHAPTER 44

On his way to Tessa's, Jerry Finlay bought two copies of the *Sun Times.* Television usually told him as much as he cared to know about what was spinning the world, but this story was a keeper. It was splashed on the front page:

Supreme Court Justice
Investigated for Murder

Judge Mark Mayfield, scheduled to be sworn in when the Supreme Court reconvenes, is in police custody and is being investigated in two homicides. Ballistic tests are expected to link the gun recovered from his yacht to the weapon used to kill his Yale University roommate, Barton Corbin. Mayfield is also a suspect in the decades old unsolved murder of Patricia Lazarus.

Scanning the rest of the lengthy article, he read, *Jerry Finlay, a private investigator, and his associate, Joyce Cole, turned over to police an incriminating letter and a Yale ring, linked to the Lazarus' murder and believed to belong to Mayfield. The valuable detective work of Nicholas Crane is credited with saving the lives of two young women and keeping the alleged murderer from taking a seat on the country's highest court.*

Jerry hoped seeing her name on the front page would please Joyce and help her forget she wouldn't be getting a share of an annuity. He was going to buy her the longest, most dangly pair of earrings he could find.

He wondered if she liked cats.

Nickolae Gerstner (Nicki Baker) served as staff writer for the Los Angeles County Office of Education and began her free-lance career writing magazine and newspaper pieces.

Her first book was an historical novel, *No Bed In Deseret*. After listening to Mary Higgins Clark give the keynote address at a writers' conference, she became intrigued with the mystery genre and launched a mystery writing career. Her mystery novels have been translated into many languages and *Finders Keepers*, co-authored with Barbara Pronin, was included in a Reader's Digest Anthology. Two of her books, Finders Keepers and Dark Veil, have been optioned for film.

A native Chicagoan, she is a graduate of the University of Illinois, Urbana campus. She and her husband, John, divide their time between homes in California and New York. Their traveling companion is a Siamese cat named Pippin.

Made in the USA
Middletown, DE
04 November 2015